**THE NEW UTOPIA
J. BILLINGS**

2023 © J. BILLINGS
ISBN: 979-8-218-30292-4
CLOAK.WTF

UTOPIA

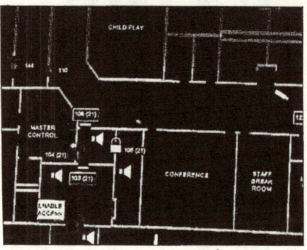

A MAN SHROUDED IN smoke a few rooms away. This is a bathhouse or it's the slum I've always lived in. Steam or opium exhaust. He whispers and the men around him laugh. I'm falling into the hairy bodice. Carlos Q whispers and they don't laugh this time. A crumpled old man in the corner has fallen asleep and his glasses slip down his nose. Carlos Q whispers again and the men have disappeared. His eyes are circled in black and blue and recessed behind a thick occipital bone, his features roll in waves, thick mountains of skin, I'm finally reaching my peak as I look at him. I think he nods in my direction; I'll never know. Two amoebas standing underwater fondle each other on a fluorescent light. The music cuts. I hear valves opening and closing, the steam shooting out in a heated moan. Carlos Q bends over and looks at the tiles between his feet. I swim to the other side of the pool and approach the steps. Water clings to me like oil. Chlorine, chlorophyll, chloroform, swirling fumes. I should be hearing the sound of dripping water, I always hear the sound of dripping water. I'll never understand the old guys who can smoke cigarettes in here. Their withered pricks are funny, though. We always laugh at them and they remain planted in place, stuck in the corners where the steam creates a thick box of shadows. Carlos Q waves me over. I can see his ribs from here and his white hairs, also black. I can't stop thinking about his bone structure. He's a long individual yet, somehow his shape morphs into a square. He's sitting on a wooden bench with his ankles in the water and a towel loosely hanging around his waist. He waved me over after the men left. He waved me over because the men are gone. They're here, here somewhere, but gone from Carlos Q. Always men with him and never men with him. Carlos Q is surrounded but alone. I come to him because he waved me over. I should sit down next to him. I should wade into the small pool at his feet. I should make him my god. I should offer myself to be baptized. I should watch him explode. I put my head under the water and the heat fizzles through my temple. I am risen and he looks at the brown Spanish tile. I wave my arms through the water. Another man walks into the pool with me. He's large and his largeness is a way of dictating ownership. Carlos Q looks at the tile. The large man hums to himself and now I can't hear the valves and the steam and the dripping and the groans and the whispers and the muted laughs and the little splashes. I like to identify the splashes. When Carlos Q drowns someone, there are no splashes. One time he told me death is peaceful, thus peace is hostile. Horrible peace, then beautiful violence. And so on, so forth, we find ourselves back to death. He never told me that. I'm not sure he ever told me that. I come out of the water and sit next to him. He looks at the faded brown tile and his body steams. His body steams like a pile of shit. He doesn't say anything. I hear him. I hear the rush of him. He is not human, he is conch. Carlos Q is a beautiful pile of clean, pristine shit and he is a whispering mollusk. The light above us flickers and I'm back in Hungary, at Gellert Bath, inside the sweaty caverns.[1] Carlos Q clears his throat. He looks at the stained brown tile. I lean back against the moist wall. Everything excretes in unison. I see his throat move. What is it Carlos Q, you steaming shit of God? I see his throat moving, I swear. I swear by my own mother. "There is an undeniable holiness to these concrete churches," he says. He is looking at the cracked brown tiles. His eyes are almost gone. His eye sockets are funnels. I want to be

---

[1] (Roque was with me. We talked about the things we thought about often. "Oedipal instincts," he said. "Do you mean you want to fuck your mother?" I asked him. I think we were in the basement at this point. "No," he said, "it has nothing to do with your mother. Not any specific mother. Just the instinctual feeling of someone wanting to fuck their mother. Not the crude reality of it. The hidden theory behind it." ... "What's the theory of wanting to fuck your mother?" ... "To re-enter the void," he said, "to become a single atom again." ... "Completion, absolution.")

submerged. The fat man is still singing and I bet this fucker wants me to tell him he's doing a good job. I step into the water again and it's cold. That's what I tell myself. I lower my head and spin away from the fat man, back towards Carlos Q. His feet are gone. I come up for air, I come up for Carlos Q. I see a stain on the wooden bench, the Rorshach blot of his ass. Carlos Q is gone and Carlos Q is still here.

Udo placed his tarot cards down in front of the keyboard and asked his partner to take a look at the Doctor pacing in front of the window. Sonya ignored him and sniffed the air for the scent of her body. The basement reminded them of themselves and they hated it.

On the fading screens to their right, the Doctor looked out into the street, watched for headlights. Nothing else to watch for.

"Do you listen to fusion jazz?"

What was that?

Screens to their left, chamomile static covered the red-headed girl's face. Alone with her freckles and never alone.

The Doctor scratched his head; he didn't seem like he could wait anymore.

So many of their forms in complete sync, the wall vibrated pointillisms, the Fraser spiral. TVs to infinity.

The detectives ate hydrogenated junk food under the high-strung decibels. The gray rug picked up their meal. The supply closet behind them was full of rats. The janitor never said a word.

Sonya had long black hair and Udo had no hair. They tried to keep track of all the things within their hate. *Sonya, Udo, Unya, Uda, Sonyo, Soo, Udoya, Udosonya. Udo's on Ya.* Faceless selves in the face of the self.

Udo often thought about interrogating the Doctor and had to admit he wouldn't be able to stop himself from asking about hair remedies. Sonya often thought about Jenny, the girl splayed over the couch, the girl alone but never alone. The detectives wondered what they would do if they saw each other on the TV screens. Sonya listening intently to the Doctor, Udo would undress. Udo upside down with the girl, Sonya would murder him.

Udo's cellphone rang and he looked at the number for six seconds before carefully placing the phone down on the table without answering.

Off-screen, from the abyss: "Stay there, I like to see you in the wind."

Jenny appeared alone but was never alone. The Doctor could be alone sometimes, although he didn't seem to like when he was. Still looking outside. He ran his hand through his gray hair. The rain in globs on his windowsill. Udo watched the Doctor very close to the screen. They were supposed to take notes. They remembered everything. Every hand, every mouth. Sonya remembered Jenny. She liked the color yellow. Her skin was pink from the sun even though she was always in the apartment when they watched her.

That's what it was, the Doctor was always waiting for something.

A few weeks ago, the detectives listened to a conversation the Doctor had with a patient who smoked codeine-dipped cigars and sat with cadavers and thought to himself for hours. He worked in the basement too. Another basement. One of many.

Someone extended a hand into the picture. The girl was a bunch of squares of red and yellow and white and dim gray. Frecklated pixels. Sonya liked to watch her.

The Doctor looked at his watch. He took a few pills. He unzipped his pants and checked himself in the mirror. He stood in the corner and rocked his head from side to side.

The girl didn't move from the couch.

Udo asked his partner to come take a look at something and she ignored him so she could keep watching the girl. Someone said something she couldn't hear. She wrote it down anyway, what she guessed they said. Never any repercussions. They thought they had been forgotten down there in the basement. They thought Jenny and the Doctor probably felt forgotten, probably wished they'd been forgotten.

Jenny raised her legs over the side of the couch.

The Doctor waved to someone on the other side of the window and left without his raincoat.

ROQUE TOLD ME, down past the bootleg chicken spot, a few blocks from the mom n' pop pharmacy, there's a warehouse with a sign that says *Mike Gray Enterprises* and inside there are thousands of crumbled computer parts stacked in tangled columns. A lone office located at the front of the building is the only room separated from the main warehouse space, but it retains the same technological detritus—wires from the ceiling and shattered micro-boards packed into every hole and crevice. In this office, there's an opening which looks like a closet but is actually a doorway leading to a set of stairs descending down a few hundred feet to a series of concrete tunnels, each slightly larger than the hull of a commercial plane, all extending outwards to additional far-off doors, opening to shrinking corridors, more doors and then stairs, possibly ascending or descending, sometimes simultaneously, eventually reaching doors again, and then another or multiple others, matryoshkian envelopes, immediately opening in or out upon each other, some conduits for the final copulation of a terminal door and others becoming impotent in their confusion, eating away at the gray areas in between, those absent of pebbly obstructions and obsolete pipes, failures in the mission of megalopolic connection. The synecdochical behemoth. An underground quagmire.

Within the belly, a tiered coliseum, periodic shows of nobody, archways backgrounded by blackness, shadows puppeteering themselves on the sandstone block canvas, seating for twenty-thousand absences, acoustics divine. Further on, marbleized salt obelisks with healing powers, undiscovered for decades, uncovered and exploited for many more, smoothed over by rubbing and wishing and kneading, proving and falsifying a primeval faith in miracles. Further still, the earth's anal cavities. But, in one corner, one of the final destinations, at the end of one of the intestinal byways, maybe just under the desolated bank building in the center of the city, the center of everything-held-dear, or possibly under a wide-open green space where the imported buffalo shit in heaping piles, there is a certain door. Closest to all of us yet furthest away. In the depths of the spider dreams. Inside this door is another door and a long hallway and then another door. The crypt is there.

Boris and Mr. Ricky in box 3, seats 14 and 15. Next to them, Boris' son's girlfriend. "Roque, do you see her?" I'm waiting for the bile of the air to hit me. Everyone is watching the son of Boris score goal after goal. "Roque, don't you think he should share a bit?" When will Son of Boris stop scoring all the goals for Le Rouge? He's going to get sent to Europe, I know it. And then what will his father do?

A BRIDGE, A PASSAGE, A RUNWAY, VIADUCT, VORTEX, a miasma in the seams, oscillation in the voices, muddy rainwater falling into the sewers, conversations fighting one another, the alien noir, the blank stares, the underworld and the overworld, the blood, the saliva, the in-between. Sonya paused. *The sinews reconnect in the microwave.*

Out of the corner of her eyes, she saw a man scan his eye with the eye of his phone. Jenny pulled him towards the street. Sonya tried to think Jenny's thoughts, find her ascension. *Bend me over the keg, preach to me about the log, venture into the cave, believe in the present, this way, around the stone corner, ignore the birds, ignore the crows, they're guffawing elsewhere, step in front of the crowd, dance in front of them, follow the beacon, we can be the beacon.*

Sonya picked out their whispers. She knew how to parse the inflections. She touched all of the metal sides to intake her residuals. Her left was her left and her right was her right and her straightforwardness became her straightforwardness.

I'm told of this city growing beyond its infrastructure, but all I see is emptiness in the houses and slow men smoking cigarettes on the crosswalks.

Jenny pulled the man across the street as if the sedan would drive through her. Sonya knew the sedan. Maybe Jenny knew the sedan too. She knew the practice of it and its habit. Steps uninterrupted, the brake pedal remained immaculate and the sedan drove on to be knowable elsewhere. Jenny moved to remain unknowable in her little white lies. The man followed her by hand onto the sidewalk. He chose Jenny. At first he did not choose Jenny and then later on he chose her and Sonya chose him as an extension of choosing Jenny.

Jenny's green dress fitted her form and her raincoat kept that form intact. He wore jeans and a suede jacket and a black ballcap. Sonya in her only clothes. The pistol abided, braced against her leg.

A duplex among the scorched apartments. Architectural parallelograms looming in the background. The steel casing, the vertebrae, the rigid steps of the fire escape. Jenny liked to walk fast. Sonya sat under a blank billboard. She liked to watch her. She liked to watch her as if everyone's fate would be decided through pictures of the unknown moments in their lives.

She thought about what she would say to her. A line from a movie. Something old fashioned. Something beautiful. She would say something with nothing, in silence, in the ultimate quietness, an arid salt flat.

Jenny pulled the man through the window of the apartment and, in Sonya's imagination, onto the bed, ass in the refrigerator, head out the window, dick floating in red gelatin, she's cleaning him off with Lysol wipes, he's paying her in a dirty glass jar full of nickels, she's taking the coins to a Coinstar at the dingiest corner store called something like Dad's Place or Peg's Vintage Beer, she's buying a packet of peppermint lozenges and a sticky bun and a diet soda, she's eating at her small circular red

Formica table in the middle of her kitchen decorated with porcelain figurines wearing Lederhosen, she's talking on the phone and swirling a lozenge in her mouth, she's sitting on the toilet while she runs the shower, she's talking on the phone again but this time with no lozenge and instead she's drinking a glass of tap water because the diet soda made her stomach feel funny, she's smoking a cigarette and blowing the smoke out her half-open window, she's talking on the phone again this time in whispers, she's watching re-runs of *Fear Factor* on TV, she's putting on a letterman's jacket and walking across the street to a park pavilion in front of a pond, she's shaking a man's hand, she's shaking another man's hand, the men shake each other's hands and admire each other's suits, they all get into a car, the car does a circle around the park, both of the men get out and start yelling at each other, the car takes off with Jenny inside, the men begin to berate each other and tell each other they'll never make business deals together again, the car circles back and a window in the front rolls down and the men stop talking immediately, the men remain silent until the window rolls back up, the car leaves and enters the vacuum of the city, the men disappear, Jenny exits the car after it pulls up to a club, she walks in unabated, she puts on headphones and listens to *Vomit* by Girls and sways slowly in the middle of the floor, she touches a few faces, she dances with a boy under the color green, she hangs her headphones around her neck and goes to the bar and talks to the bartender about pool chemicals, she drinks a light German beer and then another, she goes to the bathroom because she thinks she's getting her period but she's not, she walks past the sink without washing her hands, she goes to find the boy, they talk about old Italian movies and she says she loves them and he says he hates them but they can't hear each other over the bludgeoning music so they end up having two separate simultaneous conversations—she really loves *L'Avventura* because all of the characters are able to find peace while being miserable, or maybe it's the other way around and they're able to find things to be miserable about while they're at peace, plus they go all over the little tiny Italian towns instead of fulfilling Americans' obnoxious obsession with Rome and Milan and Venice, although she kind of loves Venice, mostly because of that one movie with Donald Sutherland, oh, Donald Sutherland, and come to think about it, those two movies are pretty similar, if you really think about it— and she's glad she can't hear the boy talking, she likes it better to see his mouth opening and closing and only hear the robotic music, and she lets the boy suck on her finger in the middle of the dance floor, she leaves an hour before the club closes so she can beat the rush, another car picks her up, no one talks, she comes home late at night and considers re-reading her favorite short story, she can't remember the title, it's about a ventriloquist's doll and it's kind of funny and it's by Shirley Jackson, but instead of reading she sits on the fire escape and drinks the rest of her diet soda before washing her face and putting on a velvet eye mask and falling asleep on the couch.

Here is the beginning of her universe.

Sonya smoked a cigarette and thought about all of the words she had heard Jenny say. All of the variations of the same thing: "XXX is the XXX of my XXX." . . . "Do you XXX?" ... "Please XXX with XXX." ... "Yes, I XXX very much." ... "I'm going to XXX." ... "XXX is beautiful and XXX is even more beautiful." ... "What is inside the XXX?" ... "Hello XXX." ... She heard her voice in the static of the old television. The static simmered into her dreams. A dream of a carnival barker carrying a whipping belt. A dream of Udo's face smiling in through the window. A dream of the cell at the station. A dream of being alone on a beach. The kind of alone where she would not be alone. Jenny's voice everywhere, embedded in the walls, shimmering through the wind, heaving into the corners and air bubbles. Jenny's words, her own, those spoken words from her own lips, becoming shared. Sonya looked down at the piece of paper in her hands and read the words she had written inside the basement: *Cohen gave up the ghost.*

Udo's wool pants clung to his body.

I can't go on caring like this.

An airplane flew into that theater during a screening of Shangri-la.

Here's the thing: discontinue the need in yourself to find definition.

An eternal need to piss. *If I step quietly enough, there will be no one here.* His prostate couldn't handle the life he had constructed.

The projector clicked like a diseased metronome. He snapped in time. He didn't know how to snap. He didn't know anyone showed Japanese films in the United States. He didn't know there was a market for such things. He didn't know such a market existed. He didn't know anything about these films. He didn't know the language. He didn't know the essence of the language. It all escaped him. His coldness and dampness resided. He thought about being underground. *I am thinking about being underground. I am thinking of being underground with her. As well as the rats. The Rat Czar says to starve them out, because if we kill them in cold blood then the survivors grow larger because they have less competition for food, but if they're starved then they begin to eat their own. Rats are limitless. Our extinction is much more likely. It's that way because we're civilized. If we ate garbage, we'd have a better chance at surviving. There is hope for me, maybe.*

On the screen, a lonely man taped a room shut and his body dissolved. The detective couldn't find reality. He wiped his forehead with a yellow handkerchief. Another character placed a plastic bag over his head and shot himself in the face. *I'm starting to feel the pulse of the movie now. What it needs to put it over the top is some bad CGI.*

Imagine sitting in a theater like this one and a plane bursts through the left wall and exits through the right wall and the movie continues. The movie will always continue.

He was starting to put his thumb on its pith. The film began to enter him. A cinematic suppository. A man with shaggy hair walked around an industrial warehouse and talked to himself. Udo tried to pretend the projector did not exist. A spontaneous appearance of these people. He wiped his forehead again and turned to the Doctor next to him.

"They say speaking fears aloud gives power, so I have to tell you I cannot stop thinking of aneurysms of all kinds."

"Who says that?"

"..."

"..."

"The lights shouldn't be this dim. Imagine what a pervert could do in here." A child let out a faint cry behind them.

"Who told you about aneurysms?"

"The internet."

On the screen, a man looked at a computer and smiled at the horrific things he saw.

"I've studied medicine all of my life and I've never heard of these things."

"Pinched optic nerves. The hose kinks and the eyeball explodes."

"Is that where you're feeling the pain?"

"I'll have you know, I'm very happy with the pain I'm feeling. I'm completely satisfied."

"..."

"..."

"I know a man who could give you a tonic for your hair. But I would be careful. Self-esteem is the richest drug in existence."

"Maybe it's too late. Even in my dreams I'm bald."

"Baldness and death are similar concepts. The elimination of self."

"I've seen you admire your prick more times than I care to say."

His rhombus.

"Why do you think I do it? I like to show off in front of the camera."

The panopticon does not work as intended if there is a desire to be watched. The effects will be reversed.

A large boat carried itself across the screen and the credits rolled and the ghosts lived on. The lights went up and the detective turned away from the Doctor's face.

"I have to piss, Doctor. I always have to piss."

"I can write you a prescription for that."

"I think that's a conflict of interest."

The Doctor shook his head. "The Devil has already made plans to escort me to Hell."

The detective left his seat and walked up the ramped concrete aisle. In the last row, a child spread limp across the laps of his parents. A child end to end. Flashlights in his eye. Examination of the red blood drop squeezing out of his cornea. They would need the police and a doctor. The detective had to piss and the Doctor would have places to go.

Mr. Ricky's boyfriend is here and he has *your valentine* tattooed across his neck and a large void in the center of his earlobe and from the void hangs an earring and on the earring's chain is a USB drive.

¶ ("I am happy being many atoms," I said. Roque told me he felt the same way, he just liked to think about the *theoretical concept*. I told him there were too many layers to this Oedipal thinking and he smiled proudly. "Something else I think about often is the most terrifying sentence in literature: *Then they went to the basement.*")

A SEAT BY THE WINDOW IN THE YOUNG PILOT'S CLUB, his roller bag next to him, watching planes leave to every place he would go but never see, Ibex Maurio. Three Penicillin scotches and two Heinekens and one shot of bland tequila and four cognacs and a black-pepper mezcal and a sip of bubblegum-flavored Benadryl and *what the hell* two banana daquiris and three glasses of Port wine and one whiskey sour and then another and one more before his fourth. The television above the bar glitched back and forth between a Catholic mass and grainy footage of a soccer match.

Everybody from the 70's is bow-legged. He unzipped his roller bag and felt around for something he knew was not there. *They can't fucking run for their flights like that. It should be illegal.* The bartender served him his glasses on white napkins with small, simplified blueprints of different airplanes.

The sky looked dark; the weather reports argued for perfect clearness. This one was off to Paris, this one was off to Berlin, this one never to be found again, this one was off to Scandinavia and then Malawi.

He stuck his hand in the matter of his bag again and swam his fingers to find the vial, which was not there. *Everyone likes pilots. There is an eternal ego. Pilot school is a culture of disease.* Two flight attendants he knew and sometimes worked with walked in and sat at the bar. That one had served him ginger ale and that one had served him stale cake wrapped in plastic. The clouds collapsed. It was nice to not be inside the air. The blue of sacred priority.

"And another one, sir?"

He ordered three more what's-it-calleds.

The flight attendants left and *how did they even fucking get in here? What is the meaning of "club"? Isn't there supposed to be dancing? Those bow-legs used to be good for something. Turn up this music,* could he ask that? The bartender turned up the television instead. *No one is dancing to this. Absolutely no one.*

He remembered the time he flew to Gibraltar. The time he played 36 holes with Agamemnon. The time he wrestled in the street with a stalker. The time he puked dried blood. The time he walked through security with a gun. The time he cried as his mother died on the phone. The time he walked in on his father.

He reached down further this time, swiping for his cocaine. The erect tower stood tall, as it always did. He knew some of the sperm inside. Good men and women. Witnesses to the endless procession.

He asked the bartender if he could have a kiwi. "The alien fruit," he said. A man with dark souls in his eyes laughed from across the club.

The thing is, there will always be another flight. He liked to read the passenger manifestos. Calksinv, Christopherq. Halloween, John Michael. Chan, Consequence. Delirious, Stanley.

He ate the kiwi like an apple. A voracious pimple.

He was supposed to be the goddamn Captain. Captain

Ibex Maurio, on duty, willing and able, ready to shatter at will, snorting the life out of itself, watching every person walk up and down the aisle in G Minor, speaking into the microphone with authority, with virality, loving on himself, flying into the unknown and returning.

"Will you be in need of service while you're in town?"

It's quite possible his ocular blood vessels have exploded.

"Yes," Ibex said.

"Have you been abandoned?"

"Yes," he said.

"Have we met before?"

"Yes," he said. He left his kiwi on the table, punished and leaking. They walked to the other side of the club and the bartender crossed himself in the direction of the television after a player in purple and yellow scored again. The counter wiped perfectly clean. The rows of bottles even and dry. The bowls of mixed nuts and mints remained rotund. Through the doorway and through another doorway and under a poster of the muddled inkjet sky.

The stone always felt cold. Always that way, always rubbing the hair off his knees.

He put on his hat because the Captain was supposed to wear his hat.

His roller bag left behind, subject to join the other million parcels of luggage emptied into the cavernous rift of the Midwest. His slacks buried beneath a perfectly mulched yard. His eczema cream eaten for breakfast next to Orange Juice and charred toast. His boxers hung as a flag at a youth sporting park.

The man in front of him was bow-legged and they walked down the stairs together.

127 Zapata Boulevard does not exist. The sequence goes: 121, 123, 125, 129, 131. Societal infrastructure places it on the same block as the Planet Jackpot Internet Café. The World Wide Web dictates its place from only a few feet away and comes up empty, droning, and missing. 125 Zapata Boulevard exists, I've been there, I stopped in a few years ago, invited off the street by the local car baron's nephew and his friends, stoned eternals, and we watched a few minutes of a basketball game before we changed the channel to a never-ending stream of informercials and I asked about their neighbors and they talked about a tall man prowling for nubile teens and intercepting them as they back-seat fucked in empty parking lots and they sweated and said "Terramania" and they blended together various fruits of the world and drank the smoothies slowly, emptied them into their throats until they almost choked, and I felt like I was watching a movie and the memory feels like a sequel, or a bad remake of the original, and when I see 125, when I am thinking of 127 again, I try to forget the memory and instead try to imagine what happened when the children of the prom emptied out into the streets at midnight. But 127 does not exist and there is no scourge left in the open where it should be, there is no "where it should be," there is no emptiness, the

fullness is its emptiness. 127 Zapata Boulevard, the imperfect system, undefinable. The pop song that has killed me. Every wormhole sucking itself off. We can smell its paint from here. We are all there, the "there" is nowhere. Nietzschean happiness solidified as gargoyled walls. If the end of the world is disappearance, 127 is the very beginning.

SHE CLOSED THE DOOR BEHIND HER and turned around and saw him and they held an unspoken race to be the first to not turn on the light.

Deep mahogany strands in the darkness, Udo's make-believe goddess. His circadian rhythm of the night clicked on, his legs opened, every confusing pore. She took off her coat and dropped it to the floor in front of the bed. Udo leaned back in his chair and gestured towards the mumbling television. "I've been watching while you were out. Soap operas. Have you ever seen *Cuckholded in the Age of Compassion?*"

She nodded her head and sat on the edge of the bed with her legs crossed.

"I've seen every episode. Every single one except the finale. Don't you think it's much more satisfying not seeing the end?" She smiled and he saw it all in her. His cigarette twitched. "What do we do with you?" he said. "What do we do with you?"

There's lots of things to do with me, she said. Of course, she didn't say that. He wanted her to. He thought she would. She wouldn't. She asked him what he would do with her and he hated the question. There was no definitiveness.

Ask me in a second. In the moment. The law is very confusing here. This is a deep gray area. The moral law is much clearer but the criminal law has become so bastardized, right and wrong are deformed incestual cousins. And moral law is a bitch anyway. "I would like to unleash the bitch in you," he said.

"Unleash the bitch in me?"

"I'm a strange man with strange ecstasies. You're not afraid of a strange man in your room in the dark?"

She didn't answer him and for a moment he wondered if she'd disappeared.

"Maybe we should talk," he said.

"I like to talk too," she said.

"If you like to talk then we should talk."

"Okay."

"Okay."

"What's on your mind?"

"My neighbor is a delirious man. He's awake at all hours of the day and night. Normally, I'm not bothered. In fact, it's nice to know I'm not the only one awake at those hours. God knows I never talk to him at 3 a.m., but it's nice to know there's someone else fucking around out there. Lately though, he has implanted himself in his yard where he yells at the top of his lungs at this awful time of night. He only yells one thing. He yells: 'Do you want to know the secret of evil?'"

"Do you want to know the secret of evil?"

"Do you want to know the secret of evil?! Do you want to know the secret of evil?! Do you want to know the secret of evil?!"

"And what is it?"

"The secret?"

"The secret."

"There's no secret."

"That's what he says?"

"No, I never answer him. I have no idea what he thinks. I just know there's no secret."

" . . . "

"I'm kidding, I take it back. If the secret is anything, it's in the blistering heat of man's hole."

My rhombus.

She laughed.

He turned his head up to the corner where the wall met the ceiling, above the potted plant, atop the wooden armoire, and he offered a wink, a fraternal wartime gesture.

"No," he shook his head. "The secret of evil must remain a secret."

"What?" she asked.

"It must remain a secret," he said, "or else there's no evil, and evil is necessary."

" . . . "

"What do you think about that?" he asked.

She looked out the window and stared at the dark sky, as if the answers were traced in the galaxy's nuclei. "I would tell him: do not fear the nightmare."

Udo stood up and stretched out. She didn't move as he took his first steps towards her. "I like my answer better." He reached down for his handcuffs and Jenny looked away.

Son of Boris scored another goal. He scored a fucking Olímpico. This place is nuts, but Boris doesn't cheer, he stands there thinking about the gun in his glove compartment. They're playing in a 5-4-1 and Son of Boris is the lone option. We're chanting *Son-of-Bo-ris-Son-of-Bo-ris*. He doesn't notice. He's not doing it for us, he's doing it for himself.

INSIDE MY DREAM, three brutalist structures speak to each other, great monuments, rejected: "There is no such thing as aesthetic, only falseness and trueness." ... "That is easy to say for an obelisk." ... "Aren't we all obelisks?" ... "We are all expired and meaningless." ... "Movements within do not give us purpose. Our structure gives us purpose." ... "You are two large discs jutting out from a mountainside. I am a blank pillar of stairs rising endlessly into the sky." ... "And I am tan and leathered above my concrete." ... "I can still feel my glass. It is not cold or jagged or smooth. It is an angle. There are degrees to its state of being." ... "Nature has not overtaken any of you. I am scalloped and open." ... "You were made that way." ... "Light mingled with the people and you were holy. You were made to be holy. You were made to be constant." ... "I was made to be felt and left." ... "They made me as a distraction." ... "You are a pilgrimage."

MEN LINED IN STALLS LIKE CATTLE. Fingers beat in stampedes. Stray moans, braying in heat. The humming of fans cushioning unretrievable plastics. Welcome to the satellite, inside the electrified air. Digitized trumpets announced the arrival of a searcher, a scholar, an improprietor, a shopper, a pregnant thief. The ancient machines boasted their age, surrounded by sour cushions and flimsy cubicle retainers. Financed capital expenditures impossible for such an establishment. Required the willingness of a bank to trust and believe in the mission. Required the withstanding of hours of coffee-injected dives under the skin of numbers representing falsified amounts printed in wisps on reams of cheap vanilla paper. Instead, the monolith supported the weight of itself, uniting the world by breaking it down into pieces attainable only for those with dexterous fingers.

He inserted a USB drive into the ass of the computer and roiled his fingers to command the absent specter to scroll through the system's labyrinthian files, root folders converging into sub-folders and sister folders, sub-folders and sister folders displacing into sub-sub-folders, sub-sub-folders devolving into sub-sub-sub folders, sub-sub-sub folders giving way to sub-sub-sub-sub-folders, sub-sub-sub-sub-folders following an exponential destiny to sub-sub-sub-sub-sub folders, sub-sub-sub-sub-sub-folders revealing trances, terrors, inspirations, dark flashes, angels. *The genealogy of Heaven.* He ate the tip of a chocolate bar sprouted from its casing and followed the morsel through his descending catacombs, into the sub-folder of his sarcophagus.

Just the possibility of booby-trap viruses makes me sweat.

A buzzer rang through the ceiling. Someone had won it big and the institution wanted its fair share. The thin metal pillars shot miles of unimpeded waveforms. A judge walked the aisles.

"One peach away from changing my entire wardrobe to all black everything."

"This place is always chunking."

Gacccccckkkkkkk.

"Anybody got a nickel?"

I'm not sure how I'll be able to counteract the damage I'm doing to my optical nerves.

The tongue of the man across from him. The tapping foot of the man next to him. The archaic scratching of the man beside that one. The stretching and aching of the man behind him. He monitored his own movements. *Morsel entering sub-sub-folder.* His feet hurt. The man behind him stretching and aching. He didn't understand the muscular tension. *Morsel entering sub-sub-sub-folder. Everything's happening too quickly.* The files organized into a scrolling womb. Lines piled on top of each other. Babel in reverse. His eyeballs spasmed in random jilts. Fingers moved without command. Inherent direction. Strands of hair in between the keys, balled and curled into hooks. Vacuum-sealed laminates penning in the grime. There is no time in the throes of electro-lust.

The clicking and tapping and striking and hitting and thudding and pressing and mashing and pushing and clattering constructed a fuzzy cocoon and he lived inside the four walls of the stanchion, his brain becoming heavier. The x-rays of the alphanumeric columns floating out from their borders into the air.

Finally, he leaned back slightly, exiting the hypnosis. The livestock garbled away. Anonymity and privacy only existed in the public sphere, as part of the whole mass. Too much to mind on one's own. Again, stretching and aching out loud behind him. He became more concerned for the well-being of this man. He imagined the man looping backwards, arching himself into a knot, just for a glance. Just for a glance. He raised his shoulders as an obstruction.

Hnnggghhhhhh. More stretching and aching.

He shoved himself in front of the blinking screen. A prompt appeared: *Do you want to continue?* The cursor became cursed. He dug the mouse into the table. An old mule grinding its hooves into the mud. *Yes, yes, yes.* Always two ways, technology always offered a back road, a trap door, a Plan B. His fingers tapped, a destitute clacking.

Agggghhhhh.

A degenerate. A phantom gymnast bending over himself. A peek, just a hit of it. Techno-addict. He whipped around to return a glance and crossed the threshold of an open-eyed gaze and the man behind him became the man in front of him, scouring his own code. Now, the man inside of him.

Within his gut, he felt the computer prompt counting down, synced to the gradual movement of the food particles towards their exit.

3.

The internal language of the man across from him was one he could not interpret or understand.

2.

If I'm only able to dream of faces I've seen in my waking hours, does that mean I cannot see faces I haven't dreamed of?

1.

The screen of the man across from him was blank, there were no signs of life, none in his eyes or his computer.

0.

The prompt dissolved into squarish bits. The commands tumbled. The gateway severed.

▌("What book is that from?" ... "I don't know. The one where all the women died from unexplained violent causes." ... "And they all died in basements?" ... "No, none of them did. That's why it's so frightening. The book was a number, let's call it *B,* and the extremism of *B's* word count got it banned from the library and when I finally found a copy of *B,* in the back, on the last page, some psycho wrote *B* + 1." ... "Trash the B. What was the number?" ... "I don't remember, but I remember the book. I lost my copy and I was disturbed and then I found a new copy and I was more disturbed. Owning a copy meant I was subject to its whims, but gaining another copy meant I would need to be scared for the world, this thing was really out there mingling in with the people and their vibrance." ... " ... " ... " ... " ... " ... " ... ")

Mr. Ricky's boyfriend is going to get food. He likes to eat chicken tenders because he's a fucking baby. The red-head is leaving too. She's seen all of her boyfriend's goals and she thinks they're all the same. Once, I saw Son of Boris buying snacks at my corner store. The red-head wasn't there. Son of Boris likes cakes. I'm leaving to buy those same cakes. I feel settled in the bile now. Roque is humping the seats behind us. "Roque, if you're going to go all the way then go all the way but if not then dismount from the chair, you beast." I traverse the endless stairs. This stadium is made of concrete.

"Right now, at this moment, the world's number one rated pinball player is a pervert." *It's a good thing they don't respond.* The room scaled with tin and aluminum harshness. Silver mirrors. Only whispers. Maybe they couldn't hear. He liked to think his voice could reach the afterlife.

I'm very slow right now.

"Anyone who likes to paddle balls and be rewarded for it is a pervert. The church says as much."

There was always the power of the name tag. The name was an invisible injection. The tin and aluminum did not absorb the smoke like other rooms. Everything trapped underground. Time trapped underground. The purple beauty in his Styrofoam cup. He leaned down towards the name tag and intercepted himself, to keep his familiarity in the comfort of the abyss. He pretended to touch his cigar to the eggshell sheet and imagined the gradual sear.

"There's an FBI investigation . . . I wish he wouldn't keep getting away with this. He's not my kind of pervert."

He lowered his cigar into the infinity pool again. The line of demarcation extended upwards. His fingers were almost in it. The cup effused a spotting. The cup menstruated psychotropics.

"His best game is The Goonies, and I think it's because he gets energized by the animatronic kids watching him."

His breath fumed. His eyes let out slight puffs. The vent clicked and breathed onto his face and the air rippled down his relaxed body. He moved his ass around in the camping chair. His own skin bumped in the cold air. He swirled his cigar around the cup. He felt like an old Catholic dipping bread into wine. Under the cover of churches with golden trim and angels hovering over trembling blood-bodies. *Just as the gifts of the altar are prepared, so we prepare ourselves to enter into the great blessing, the holy meal, the big swallow, the soaking, the beautiful death of self and rebirth of being, the fondling of hygienics, the carcinogenic girth of the body.* He bent down to pet his Bulldog and forgot he never had a Bulldog. *Betsy would be her name.* He picked up the Styrofoam cup and looked inside and saw the empty white tomb and looked at his nubbed cigar and slowly turned his head back to the cup and bent forward and stole a delicate bite. He chewed and tasted the crunchy dark violet fuse and swallowed and pushed the crumbling molecules down his throat with another breath of the cigar. The tin and aluminum sharpened. The drawers held fast. Everything was still. The still was everything, everything he believed in. *Thou Holy Drugs.*

"The pervert believes he can keep everything hidden away in his basement . . . I don't even know if he has a basement . . . He should have a basement if he'd like to stay hidden . . . He's been number one for three years and his son is the only one who can dethrone him . . . They do have a basement. They have forty-three pinball machines in the basement. I heard it on NPR. It's a maze of mechanized stutters and circus noises. He and his son eat peanut butter and jelly after peanut butter and jelly. They press the buttons as one touches the soft spot of a baby's skull. And yet, everyone will be surprised when they find out he's a pervert . . . He locks himself in his basement and hopes he stays trapped . . . A pervert who wishes to be trapped."

His voice entered the drawers and navigated the limbs and fell upon the body in front of him, the body with a name but no name, a lost name. His eyes followed the miniscule green light on the end of every electrical source. This would be a long night and he made it longer. He would go to his friends and all of the people who had no names and he would make them laugh and he would think about himself and his happy place in the basement next to the bodies where life moved slow and the quiet calmed him and made him feel an appropriate amount of fear.

"Carlos, Carlos."

He tried to blink.

"Carlos, Carlos."

He tried to blink.

"Carlos, Carlos."

Too neon to continue.

"Carlos, Carlos."

. . .

"Carlos."

. . .

"Carlos."

Finally. The body speaks.

```
                         [PLANETJACKPOT_7@iMac-G3 - % cd EXT_DRIVE
                         [PLANETJACKPOT_7@iMac-G3 - EXT_DRIVE % ls
STORIA          STORIB          STORIC
STORID          STORIE          STORIF
STORIG          STORIH          STORII
STORIJ          STORIK          STORIL
STORIM          STORIN          STORIO
STORIP          STORIR          STORIS
STORIT          STORIU          STORIV
STORIW          STORIX          STORIY
STORIZ
                    [PLANETJACKPOT_7@iMac-G3 EXT_DRIVE % cd STORIA
                         [PLANETJACKPOT_7@iMac-G3 - STORIA % ls
BEBA_1          BEBA_2          BUEL_1
BUEL_2          ELLE_1          ELLE_2
INGEBORG_1      INGEBORG_2      VIOLET_1
VIOLET_2
                    [PLANETJACKPOT_7@iMac-G3 STORIA % cd BEBA_1
                         [PLANETJACKPOT_7@iMac-G3 - BEBA_1 % ls
DES             EMERSON         SYLVAN
ZACHARY

                    [PLANETJACKPOT_7@iMac-G3 BEBA_1 % cd . . .
                    [PLANETJACKPOT_7@iMac-G3 STORIA % cd BUEL_1
                         [PLANETJACKPOT_7@iMac-G3 - BUEL_1 % ls
ABOURABI        BUCK            GORDON
NEFF            TITUS
                    [PLANETJACKPOT_7@iMac-G3 BUEL_1 % cd  . . .
                    [PLANETJACKPOT_7@iMac-G3 STORIA % cd ELLE_1
                         [PLANETJACKPOT_7@iMac-G3 - ELLE_1 % ls
                                                        DREAMER
                    [PLANETJACKPOT_7@iMac-G3 ELLE_1 % cd . . .
                 [PLANETJACKPOT_7@iMac-G3 STORIA % cd INGEBORG_1
                      [PLANETJACKPOT_7@iMac-G3 - INGEBORG_1 % ls
HOLLAND         LEO             NICOLETTO
REBUS
                  [PLANETJACKPOT_7@iMac-G3 INGEBORG % cd  . . .
                   [PLANETJACKPOT_7@iMac-G3 STORIA % cd VIOLET_1
                         [PLANETJACKPOT_7@iMac-G3 - VIOLET_1 % ls
EARVIN          FRIEND
                    [PLANETJACKPOT_7@iMac-G3 VIOLET_1 % cd  . . .
                    [PLANETJACKPOT_7@iMac-G3 STORIA % cd   . . .
                   [PLANETJACKPOT_7@iMac-G3 EXT_DRIVE % cd STORIB
                         [PLANETJACKPOT_7@iMac-G3 - STORIB % ls
ASYMPTOTE_1     ASYMPTOTE_2     FLORENCE_1
FLORENCE_2      KIM_1           KIM_2
                  [PLANETJACKPOT_7@iMac-G3 STORIB % cd ASYMPTOTE_1
                      [PLANETJACKPOT_7@iMac-G3 - ASYMPTOTE_1 % ls
THE_GOD_OF_ANGLES
[PLANETJACKPOT_7@iMac-G3 ASYMPTOTE_1 % cd  . . .
[PLANETJACKPOT_7@iMac-G3 STORIB % cd FLORENCE_1
[PLANETJACKPOT_7@iMac-G3 - FLORENCE_1 % ls
                                GOETHE          JULIAN
```

```
[PLANETJACKPOT_7@iMac-G3 FLORENCE_1 % cd . . .
[PLANETJACKPOT_7@iMac-G3 STORIB % cd KIM_1
[PLANETJACKPOT_7@iMac-G3 - KIM_1 % ls
                        CORBIN              ISAAC               KURT
[PLANETJACKPOT_7@iMac-G3 KIM_1 % cd . . .
[PLANETJACKPOT_7@iMac-G3 STORIB % cd . . .
[PLANETJACKPOT_7@iMac-G3 EXT_DRIVE % cd STORIC
[PLANETJACKPOT_7@iMac-G3 - STORIC % ls
            NADIA_1             NADIA_2             THEODORA_1
            THEODORA_2          ULALLA_1            ULALLA_2
                                XOL_1               XOL_2
[PLANETJACKPOT_7@iMac-G3 STORIC % cd NADIA_1
[PLANETJACKPOT_7@iMac-G3 - NADIA_1 % ls
KURT        LAIRD
[PLANETJACKPOT_7@iMac-G3 NADIA_1 % cd . . .
[PLANETJACKPOT_7@iMac-G3 STORIC % cd THEODORA_1
[PLANETJACKPOT_7@iMac-G3 - THEODORA_1 % ls
            ALAIN_DELON         BJORG               HOMER
            HOWARD              KEENE               THADDEUS
            TURNER              ULF                 XANDER
                                                    YURI
[PLANETJACKPOT_7@iMac-G3 THEODORA_1 % cd . . .
[PLANETJACKPOT_7@iMac-G3 STORIC % cd ULALLA_1
[PLANETJACKPOT_7@iMac-G3 - ULALLA_1 % ls
                                ROMERO              ZARAGOZA
[PLANETJACKPOT_7@iMac-G3 ULALLA_1 % cd . . .
[PLANETJACKPOT_7@iMac-G3 STORIC % cd XOL_1
[PLANETJACKPOT_7@iMac-G3 - XOL_1 % ls
                FATU                HORATIO             IBEX
[PLANETJACKPOT_7@iMac-G3 XOL_1 % cd . . .
[PLANETJACKPOT_7@iMac-G3 STORIC_1 % cd . . .
[PLANETJACKPOT_7@iMac-G3 EXT_DRIVE % cd STORID
[PLANETJACKPOT_7@iMac-G3 - STORID % ls
                CAT_1               CAT_2               MARGOT_1
                MARGOT_2            MISSY_1             MISSY_2
[PLANETJACKPOT_7@iMac-G3 STORID % cd CAT_1
[PLANETJACKPOT_7@iMac-G3 - CAT_1 % ls
GARDEN
[PLANETJACKPOT_7@iMac-G3 CAT_1 % cd . . .
[PLANETJACKPOT_7@iMac-G3 STORID % cd MARGOT_1
[PLANETJACKPOT_7@iMac-G3 - MARGOT_1 % ls
                    COHEN               HENRIC              WALLY
            [PLANETJACKPOT_7@iMac-G3 MARGOT_1 % cd . . .
                [PLANETJACKPOT_7@iMac-G3 STORID % cd MISSY_1
                    [PLANETJACKPOT_7@iMac-G3 - MISSY_1 % ls
BORIS       MALCOLM         SM
                [PLANETJACKPOT_7@iMac-G3 MISSY_1 % cd . . .
                [PLANETJACKPOT_7@iMac-G3 STORID % cd . . .
            [PLANETJACKPOT_7@iMac-G3 EXT_DRIVE % cd STORIE
                [PLANETJACKPOT_7@iMac-G3 - STORIE % ls
                                <<NO CONTENTS FOUND>>
                [PLANETJACKPOT_7@iMac-G3 STORIE % cd . . .
```

```
                    [PLANETJACKPOT_7@iMac-G3 EXT_DRIVE % cd STORIF
                        [PLANETJACKPOT_7@iMac-G3 - STORIF % ls
DIONYSIA_1      DIONYSIA_2      ESME_1
ESME_2          LIANA_1         LIANA_2
OMA_1           OMA_2           PHOEBE_1
PHOEBE_2        WINNIE_1        WINNIE_2
                    [PLANETJACKPOT_7@iMac-G3 STORIF % cd DIONYSIA_1
                        [PLANETJACKPOT_7@iMac-G3 - DIONYSIA_1 % ls
GOGOL           ULF
                    [PLANETJACKPOT_7@iMac-G3 DIONYSIA_1 % cd . . .
                        [PLANETJACKPOT_7@iMac-G3 STORIF % cd ESME_1
                            [PLANETJACKPOT_7@iMac-G3 - ESME_1 % ls
OLEKSANDER      RUDOLF          TUME
VICIOUS

                    [PLANETJACKPOT_7@iMac-G3 ESME_1 % cd . . .
                        [PLANETJACKPOT_7@iMac-G3 STORIF % cd LIANA_1
                            [PLANETJACKPOT_7@iMac-G3 - LIANA_1 % ls
                                                                    ALBERT
                    [PLANETJACKPOT_7@iMac-G3 LIANA_1 % cd . . .
                        [PLANETJACKPOT_7@iMac-G3 STORIF % cd OMA_1
                            [PLANETJACKPOT_7@iMac-G3 - OMA_1 % ls
CLAUDE          LEMUEL
                    [PLANETJACKPOT_7@iMac-G3 OMA_1 % cd . . .
                        [PLANETJACKPOT_7@iMac-G3 STORIF % cd PHOEBE_1
                            [PLANETJACKPOT_7@iMac-G3 - PHOEBE_1 % ls
HAL             VERNON          VOLKS
                    [PLANETJACKPOT_7@iMac-G3 PHOEBE_1 % cd . . .
                        [PLANETJACKPOT_7@iMac-G3 STORIF % cd WINNIE_1
                            [PLANETJACKPOT_7@iMac-G3 - WINNIE_1 % ls
BO              DEANGELO        MISSOURI X
                    [PLANETJACKPOT_7@iMac-G3 WINNIE_1 % cd . . .
                        [PLANETJACKPOT_7@iMac-G3 STORIF % cd . . .
                    [PLANETJACKPOT_7@iMac-G3 EXT_DRIVE % cd STORIG
                        [PLANETJACKPOT_7@iMac-G3 - STORIG % ls
ATHENA_1        ATHENA_2        DREAMER_1
DREAMER_2       INDIGO_1        INDIGO_2
OPAL_1          OPAL_2
[PLANETJACKPOT_7@iMac-G3 STORIG % cd ATHENA_1
[PLANETJACKPOT_7@iMac-G3 - ATHENA_1 % ls
PUTSCH
[PLANETJACKPOT_7@iMac-G3 ATHENA_1 % cd . . .
[PLANETJACKPOT_7@iMac-G3 STORIG % cd DREAMER_1
[PLANETJACKPOT_7@iMac-G3 - DREAMER_1 % ls
                        DAMON                   LARSON
[PLANETJACKPOT_7@iMac-G3 DREAMER_1 % cd . . .
[PLANETJACKPOT_7@iMac-G3 STORIG % cd INDIGO_1
[PLANETJACKPOT_7@iMac-G3 - INDIGO_1 % ls
                        AZTEC           COHEN           WAD
[PLANETJACKPOT_7@iMac-G3 INDIGO_1 % cd . . .
[PLANETJACKPOT_7@iMac-G3 STORIG % cd OPAL_1
[PLANETJACKPOT_7@iMac-G3 - OPAL_1 % ls
ZARAGOZA
```

```
[PLANETJACKPOT_7@iMac-G3 OPAL_1 % cd  . . .
[PLANETJACKPOT_7@iMac-G3 STORIG % cd  . . .
[PLANETJACKPOT_7@iMac-G3 EXT_DRIVE % cd STORIH
[PLANETJACKPOT_7@iMac-G3 - STORIH % ls
            BRIANNA_1           BRIANNA_2            PJ_1  PJ_2
[PLANETJACKPOT_7@iMac-G3 STORIH % cd BRIANNA_1
[PLANETJACKPOT_7@iMac-G3 - BRIANNA_1 % ls
                                        IBEX            IBEZ
[PLANETJACKPOT_7@iMac-G3 BRIANNA_1 % cd  . . .
[PLANETJACKPOT_7@iMac-G3 STORIH % cd PJ_1
[PLANETJACKPOT_7@iMac-G3 - PJ_1 % ls
                  DEVIN             GOGOL             RANUS
[PLANETJACKPOT_7@iMac-G3 PJ_1 % cd  . . .
[PLANETJACKPOT_7@iMac-G3 STORIH % cd  . . .
[PLANETJACKPOT_7@iMac-G3 EXT_DRIVE % cd STORII
[PLANETJACKPOT_7@iMac-G3 - STORII % ls
            FATIMA_1            FATIMA_2          MIRACLE_1
            MIRACLE_2           RAQUEL_1          RAQUEL_2
            UMA_1               UMA_2             V_1  V_2
[PLANETJACKPOT_7@iMac-G3 STORII % cd FATIMA_1
[PLANETJACKPOT_7@iMac-G3 - FATIMA_1 % ls
                  DALE              TORGID            ZENITH
[PLANETJACKPOT_7@iMac-G3 FATIMA_1 % cd  . . .
[PLANETJACKPOT_7@iMac-G3 STORII % cd MIRACLE_1
[PLANETJACKPOT_7@iMac-G3 - MIRACLE_1 % ls
                    B                COHEN           KURT SM
[PLANETJACKPOT_7@iMac-G3 MIRACLE_1 % cd  . . .
[PLANETJACKPOT_7@iMac-G3 STORII % cd RAQUEL_1
[PLANETJACKPOT_7@iMac-G3 - RAQUEL_1 % ls
                    BJORG             IMI             KANATA
                    PUTSCH            ULF             YI
                                                      ZARAGOZA
[PLANETJACKPOT_7@iMac-G3 RAQUEL_1 % cd  . . .
[PLANETJACKPOT_7@iMac-G3 STORII % cd UMA_1
[PLANETJACKPOT_7@iMac-G3 - UMA_1 % ls
PEREZ
[PLANETJACKPOT_7@iMac-G3 UMA_1 % cd  . . .
[PLANETJACKPOT_7@iMac-G3 STORII % cd V_1
[PLANETJACKPOT_7@iMac-G3 - V_1 % ls
                                         SM            VOELLER
[PLANETJACKPOT_7@iMac-G3 V_1 % cd  . . .
[PLANETJACKPOT_7@iMac-G3 STORII % cd  . . .
[PLANETJACKPOT_7@iMac-G3 EXT_DRIVE % cd STORIJ
[PLANETJACKPOT_7@iMac-G3 - STORIJ % ls
                    WLADYSLAWA_1                  WLADYSLAWA_2
[PLANETJACKPOT_7@iMac-G3 STORIJ % cd WLADYSLAWA_1
[PLANETJACKPOT_7@iMac-G3 - WLADYSLAWA_1 % ls
                                    HERCULES            ZEUS
[PLANETJACKPOT_7@iMac-G3 WLADYSLAWA_1 % cd  . . .
[PLANETJACKPOT_7@iMac-G3 STORIJ % cd  . . .
[PLANETJACKPOT_7@iMac-G3 EXT_DRIVE % cd STORIK
[PLANETJACKPOT_7@iMac-G3 - STORIK % ls
```

```
                    GRECIA_1            GRECIA_2              LORELAI_1
                    LORELAI_2           NADIA2_1              NADIA2_2
[PLANETJACKPOT_7@iMac-G3 STORIK % cd GRECIA_1
[PLANETJACKPOT_7@iMac-G3 - GRECIA_1 % ls
                    AGNEW               GOGOL                 JEROME
                                        MOTHERLUNT            STAPE
[PLANETJACKPOT_7@iMac-G3 GRECIA_1 % cd ...
[PLANETJACKPOT_7@iMac-G3 STORIK % cd LORELAI_1
[PLANETJACKPOT_7@iMac-G3 - LORELAI_1 % ls
                    HAL                 JOEL                  TOM
[PLANETJACKPOT_7@iMac-G3 LORELAI_1 % cd ...
[PLANETJACKPOT_7@iMac-G3 STORIK % cd NADIA2_1
[PLANETJACKPOT_7@iMac-G3 - NADIA2_1 % ls
                    KURT                LORD                  OZ
                                        SPURGEON              X
[PLANETJACKPOT_7@iMac-G3 NADIA2_1 % cd ...
[PLANETJACKPOT_7@iMac-G3 STORIK % cd ...
[PLANETJACKPOT_7@iMac-G3 EXT_DRIVE % cd STORIL
[PLANETJACKPOT_7@iMac-G3 - STORIL % ls
                    KODY_1              KODY_2                PARABOLA_1
                                                              PARABOLA_2
[PLANETJACKPOT_7@iMac-G3 STORIL % cd KODY_1
[PLANETJACKPOT_7@iMac-G3 - KODY_1 % ls
SYDNEY
[PLANETJACKPOT_7@iMac-G3 KODY_1 % cd ...
[PLANETJACKPOT_7@iMac-G3 STORIL % cd PARABOLA_1
[PLANETJACKPOT_7@iMac-G3 - PARABOLA_1 % ls
                                        DICK                  GRAY
[PLANETJACKPOT_7@iMac-G3 PARABOLA_1 % cd ...
[PLANETJACKPOT_7@iMac-G3 STORIL % cd ...
[PLANETJACKPOT_7@iMac-G3 EXT_DRIVE % cd STORIM
[PLANETJACKPOT_7@iMac-G3 - STORIM % ls
                    CORELLIA_1          CORELLIA_2            TEEMI_1
                    TEEMI_2             ZAMA_1                ZAMA_2
[PLANETJACKPOT_7@iMac-G3 STORIM % cd CORELLIA_1
[PLANETJACKPOT_7@iMac-G3 - CORELLIA_1 % ls
                    ELISHA              HAWTHORNE             LUX
[PLANETJACKPOT_7@iMac-G3 CORELLIA_1 % cd ...
[PLANETJACKPOT_7@iMac-G3 STORIM % cd TEEMI_1
[PLANETJACKPOT_7@iMac-G3 - TEEMI_1 % ls
                    ALTE                CARL                  DAWSON
[PLANETJACKPOT_7@iMac-G3 TEEMI_1 % cd ...
[PLANETJACKPOT_7@iMac-G3 STORIM % cd ZAMA_1
[PLANETJACKPOT_7@iMac-G3 - ZAMA_1 % ls
                                        GAZE                  ION
[PLANETJACKPOT_7@iMac-G3 ZAMA_1 % cd ...
[PLANETJACKPOT_7@iMac-G3 STORIM % cd ...
[PLANETJACKPOT_7@iMac-G3 EXT_DRIVE % cd STORIN
[PLANETJACKPOT_7@iMac-G3 - STORIN % ls
                    IVEY_1              IVEY_2                JENNY_1
                    JENNY_2             SUKI_1                SUKI_2
                                        VICTORIA_1            VICTORIA_2
```

```
[PLANETJACKPOT_7@iMac-G3 STORIN % cd IVEY_1
[PLANETJACKPOT_7@iMac-G3 - IVEY_1 % ls
                        JALEN           MAX             REX
[PLANETJACKPOT_7@iMac-G3 IVEY_1 % cd . . .
[PLANETJACKPOT_7@iMac-G3 STORIN % cd JENNY_1
[PLANETJACKPOT_7@iMac-G3 - JENNY_1 % ls
                        COHEN           KOSMOS          MISTER
        NIJS            UDO                             VICIOUS WADE
[PLANETJACKPOT_7@iMac-G3 JENNY_1 % cd . . .
[PLANETJACKPOT_7@iMac-G3 STORIN % cd SUKI_1
[PLANETJACKPOT_7@iMac-G3 - SUKI_1 % ls
        ANTHONY         EXCLAVE                         KURT LARSON
[PLANETJACKPOT_7@iMac-G3 SUKI_1 % cd . . .
[PLANETJACKPOT_7@iMac-G3 STORIN % cd VICTORIA_1
[PLANETJACKPOT_7@iMac-G3 - VICTORIA_1 % ls
                        FARAGUT_FARRAGUT                PIERRE
[PLANETJACKPOT_7@iMac-G3 VICTORIA_1 % cd . . .
[PLANETJACKPOT_7@iMac-G3 STORIN % cd . . .
[PLANETJACKPOT_7@iMac-G3 EXT_DRIVE % cd STORIO
[PLANETJACKPOT_7@iMac-G3 - STORIO % ls
                DIANE_1                 DIANE_2         FOLEY_1
                FOLEY_2                 VERTIGO_1       VERTIGO_2
[PLANETJACKPOT_7@iMac-G3 STORIO % cd DIANE_1
[PLANETJACKPOT_7@iMac-G3 - DIANE_1 % ls
                                BROTHER         EPISCOPANT
[PLANETJACKPOT_7@iMac-G3 DIANE_1 % cd . . .
[PLANETJACKPOT_7@iMac-G3 STORIO % cd FOLEY_1
[PLANETJACKPOT_7@iMac-G3 - FOLEY_1 % ls
                                CLEVELAND               PUTSCH
[PLANETJACKPOT_7@iMac-G3 FOLEY_1 % cd . . .
[PLANETJACKPOT_7@iMac-G3 STORIO % cd VERTIGO_1
[PLANETJACKPOT_7@iMac-G3 - VERTIGO_1 % ls
                                DEATHCOCK               MOLLOCH
[PLANETJACKPOT_7@iMac-G3 VERTIGO_1 % cd . . .
[PLANETJACKPOT_7@iMac-G3 STORIO % cd . . .
[PLANETJACKPOT_7@iMac-G3 EXT_DRIVE % cd STORIP
[PLANETJACKPOT_7@iMac-G3 - STORIP % ls
                JANET_1                 JANET_1         JESSICA_1
                JEWEL_1                 JEWEL_2         JONNY_1
                JONNY_2                 JULES_1         JULES_2
[PLANETJACKPOT_7@iMac-G3 STORIP % cd JANET_1
[PLANETJACKPOT_7@iMac-G3 - JANET_1 % ls
                        HALE            PI_MEN          ULF
[PLANETJACKPOT_7@iMac-G3 JANET_1 % cd . . .
[PLANETJACKPOT_7@iMac-G3 STORIP % cd JESSICA_1
[PLANETJACKPOT_7@iMac-G3 - JESSICA_1 % ls
THE_TWINS
[PLANETJACKPOT_7@iMac-G3 JESSICA_1 % cd . . .
[PLANETJACKPOT_7@iMac-G3 STORIP % cd JEWEL_1
[PLANETJACKPOT_7@iMac-G3 - JEWEL_1 % ls
                                        MOSES           SM
[PLANETJACKPOT_7@iMac-G3 JEWEL_1 % cd . . .
```

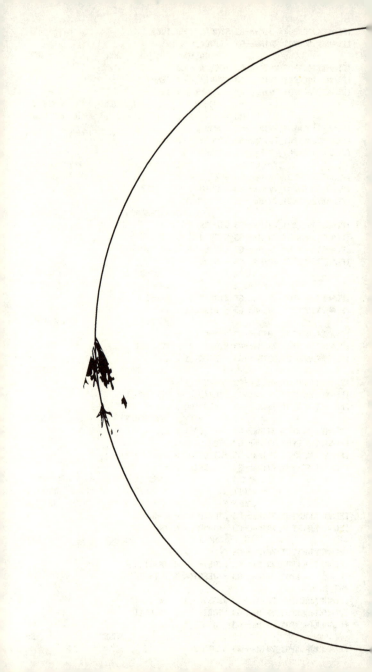

```
[PLANETJACKPOT_7@iMac-G3 STORIP % cd JONNY_1
[PLANETJACKPOT_7@iMac-G3 - JONNY_1 % ls
                                BECKER              TOKEN
[PLANETJACKPOT_7@iMac-G3 JONNY_1 % cd ...
[PLANETJACKPOT_7@iMac-G3 STORIP % cd JULES_1
[PLANETJACKPOT_7@iMac-G3 - JULES_1 % ls
               MISHITA              NOLE            RENUS REX
[PLANETJACKPOT_7@iMac-G3 JULES_1 % cd ...
[PLANETJACKPOT_7@iMac-G3 STORIP % cd ...
[PLANETJACKPOT_7@iMac-G3 EXT_DRIVE % cd STORIR
[PLANETJACKPOT_7@iMac-G3 - STORIR % ls
                                ISCHA_1             ISCHA_2
[PLANETJACKPOT_7@iMac-G3 STORIR % cd ISCHA_1
[PLANETJACKPOT_7@iMac-G3 - ISCHA_1 % ls
               LOWNDES              PLUMES          RETINA
[PLANETJACKPOT_7@iMac-G3 ISCHA_1 % cd ...
[PLANETJACKPOT_7@iMac-G3 STORIR % cd ...
[PLANETJACKPOT_7@iMac-G3 EXT_DRIVE % cd STORIS
[PLANETJACKPOT_7@iMac-G3 - STORIS % ls
          TERESA_1           TERESA_2           ZOETEMEQUE_1
                                                 ZOETEMEQUE_2
[PLANETJACKPOT_7@iMac-G3 STORIS % cd TERESA_1
[PLANETJACKPOT_7@iMac-G3 - TERESA_1 % ls
                          GOGOL         KAJ           VAN
[PLANETJACKPOT_7@iMac-G3 TERESA_1 % cd ...
[PLANETJACKPOT_7@iMac-G3 STORIS % cd ZOETEMEQUE_1
[PLANETJACKPOT_7@iMac-G3 - ZOETEMEQUE_1 % ls
                                       HJ          ZYGOTE
[PLANETJACKPOT_7@iMac-G3 ZOETEMEQUE_1 % cd ...
[PLANETJACKPOT_7@iMac-G3 STORIS % cd ...
[PLANETJACKPOT_7@iMac-G3 EXT_DRIVE % cd STORIT
[PLANETJACKPOT_7@iMac-G3 - STORIT % ls
                     AN_1              AN_2            CYRIL_1
               CYRIL_2           HEAVEN_1           HEAVEN_2
                                  YAYA_1             YAYA_2
[PLANETJACKPOT_7@iMac-G3 STORIT % cd AN_1
[PLANETJACKPOT_7@iMac-G3 - AN_1 % ls
                                COPELAND            HAMID
[PLANETJACKPOT_7@iMac-G3 AN_1 % cd ...
[PLANETJACKPOT_7@iMac-G3 STORIT % cd CYRIL_1
[PLANETJACKPOT_7@iMac-G3 - CYRIL_1 % ls
ANTHONY            ERNST             EZEKIEL KNUTE
[PLANETJACKPOT_7@iMac-G3 CYRIL_1 % cd ...
[PLANETJACKPOT_7@iMac-G3 STORIT % cd HEAVEN_1
[PLANETJACKPOT_7@iMac-G3 - HEAVEN_1 % ls
                                BJORG          BORIS         CARL
                                       COHEN         KURT          REX
                          SM              ULF          VICIOUS
[PLANETJACKPOT_7@iMac-G3 HEAVEN_1 % cd ...
[PLANETJACKPOT_7@iMac-G3 STORIT % cd YAYA_1
[PLANETJACKPOT_7@iMac-G3 - YAYA_1 % ls
RATIBOR
```

```
[PLANETJACKPOT_70iMac-G3 YAYA_1 % cd   . . .
[PLANETJACKPOT_70iMac-G3 STORIT % cd   . . .
[PLANETJACKPOT_70iMac-G3 EXT_DRIVE % cd STORIU
[PLANETJACKPOT_70iMac-G3 - STORIU % ls
                JOSIE_1             JOSIE_2             PENELOPE_1
                PENELOPE_2          REGINA_1            REGINA_2
                                    ZELDA_1             ZELDA_2
[PLANETJACKPOT_70iMac-G3 STORIU % cd JOSIE_1
[PLANETJACKPOT_70iMac-G3 - JOSIE_1 % ls
                        BIGSBY          CARL            JONHUNTER
[PLANETJACKPOT_70iMac-G3 JOSIE_1 % cd   . . .
[PLANETJACKPOT_70iMac-G3 STORIU % cd PENELOPE_1
[PLANETJACKPOT_70iMac-G3 - PENELOPE_1 % ls
                        ALTE            KEPLER          FARGAS
                                        REMUS           ZARAGOZA
[PLANETJACKPOT_70iMac-G3 PENELOPE_1 % cd   . . .
[PLANETJACKPOT_70iMac-G3 STORIU % cd REGINA_1
[PLANETJACKPOT_70iMac-G3 - REGINA_1 % ls
                                        BORIS           ELIJAH
[PLANETJACKPOT_70iMac-G3 REGINA_1 % cd   . . .
[PLANETJACKPOT_70iMac-G3 STORIU % cd ZELDA_1
[PLANETJACKPOT_70iMac-G3 - ZELDA_1 % ls
XENIUS
[PLANETJACKPOT_70iMac-G3 ZELDA_1 % cd   . . .
[PLANETJACKPOT_70iMac-G3 STORIU % cd   . . .
[PLANETJACKPOT_70iMac-G3 EXT_DRIVE % cd STORIV
[PLANETJACKPOT_70iMac-G3 - STORIV % ls
                                    SILENCE_1           SILENCE_2
[PLANETJACKPOT_70iMac-G3 STORIV % cd SILENCE_1
[PLANETJACKPOT_70iMac-G3 - SILENCE_1 % ls
X
[PLANETJACKPOT_70iMac-G3 SILENCE_1 % cd   . . .
[PLANETJACKPOT_70iMac-G3 STORIV % cd   . . .
[PLANETJACKPOT_70iMac-G3 EXT_DRIVE % cd STORIW
[PLANETJACKPOT_70iMac-G3 - STORIW % ls
                GIA_1               GIA_2               HOLLY_1
                HOLLY_2             YONA_1              YONA_2
[PLANETJACKPOT_70iMac-G3 STORIW % cd GIA_1
[PLANETJACKPOT_70iMac-G3 - GIA_1 % ls
                        CADE            KURT            VICIOUS
[PLANETJACKPOT_70iMac-G3 GIA_1 % cd   . . .
[PLANETJACKPOT_70iMac-G3 STORIW % cd HOLLY_1
[PLANETJACKPOT_70iMac-G3 - HOLLY_1 % ls
                                        KENARD          JOSKO
[PLANETJACKPOT_70iMac-G3 HOLLY_1 % cd   . . .
[PLANETJACKPOT_70iMac-G3 STORIW % cd YONA_1
[PLANETJACKPOT_70iMac-G3 - YONA_1 % ls
                LARSON              SPIRO               SUPERNOVA
                                                        WARDOG
[PLANETJACKPOT_70iMac-G3 YONA_1 % cd   . . .
[PLANETJACKPOT_70iMac-G3 STORIW % cd   . . .
[PLANETJACKPOT_70iMac-G3 EXT_DRIVE % cd STORIX
```

```
[PLANETJACKPOT_7@iMac-G3 - STORIX % ls
          SUSANA_1           SUSANA_2                    SOMNAMBULIST_1
                                                        SOMNAMBULIST_2
[PLANETJACKPOT_7@iMac-G3 STORIX % cd SUSANA_1
[PLANETJACKPOT_7@iMac-G3 - SUSANA_1 % ls
          JEREMIAH           JOSIAH                      REBUS SCHON
[PLANETJACKPOT_7@iMac-G3 SUSANA_1 % cd . . .
[PLANETJACKPOT_7@iMac-G3 STORIX % cd SOMNAMBULIST_1
[PLANETJACKPOT_7@iMac-G3 - SOMNAMBULIST_1 % ls
UDO
[PLANETJACKPOT_7@iMac-G3 SOMNAMBULIST_1 % cd . . .
[PLANETJACKPOT_7@iMac-G3 STORIX % cd . . .
[PLANETJACKPOT_7@iMac-G3 EXT_DRIVE % cd STORIY
[PLANETJACKPOT_7@iMac-G3 - STORIY % ls
```



```
                  LOW_1              LOW_2              NORI_1 NORI_2
[PLANETJACKPOT_7@iMac-G3 STORIY % cd LOW_1
[PLANETJACKPOT_7@iMac-G3 - LOW_1 % ls
COHEN
[PLANETJACKPOT_7@iMac-G3 LOW_1 % cd . . .
[PLANETJACKPOT_7@iMac-G3 STORIY % cd NORI_1
[PLANETJACKPOT_7@iMac-G3 - NORI_1 % ls
                                            KENT            PLANET
[PLANETJACKPOT_7@iMac-G3 NORI_1 % cd . . .
[PLANETJACKPOT_7@iMac-G3 STORIY % cd . . .
[PLANETJACKPOT_7@iMac-G3 EXT_DRIVE % cd STORIZ
[PLANETJACKPOT_7@iMac-G3 - STORIZ % ls
            HANNA_1            HANNA_2              XENIA_1 XENIA_2
[PLANETJACKPOT_7@iMac-G3 STORIZ % cd HANNA_1
[PLANETJACKPOT_7@iMac-G3 - HANNA_1 % ls
                                            RANUS              REX
[PLANETJACKPOT_7@iMac-G3 HANNA_1 % cd . . .
[PLANETJACKPOT_7@iMac-G3 STORIZ % cd XENIA_1
[PLANETJACKPOT_7@iMac-G3 - XENIA_1 % ls
                              OH              SM              YELLOW
```

I KNOW A LEGEND OF HELL. Where the streets widen into darkness. According to Roque, a sect of demons guards the outer rim of an occult crater and, within this sect, one specific demon called Binks found out he could take a peek at Heaven if he lifted up a certain misshapen rock on the edge of the crater. Paradise, inarguably majestic. Some demons thought their eyes wouldn't be able to take it, but they were wrong, they could, and Binks couldn't look away. He watched nirvanic souls weep at Heaven's entrance and the tears taught him about the thin line between pain and happiness. He heard screams coming from Heaven at all hours of the eternal night, beautiful sounds to his ears, no idea the screams were being prompted in worship, not fear. At first, Binks never considered trying to escape. He knew his appropriate place was in Hell, like every good little demon. But eventually he came up with an idea: to merge Heaven and Hell, to combine pain and happiness into a single galactic orifice. The Devil found out almost immediately, because demons are ferocious gossipers, and Satan banished Binks from Hell. St. Peter offered to take Binks in, and he happily accepted, whereupon he immediately withered and died. The Devil cried over him and Jesus wept. After all, everyone is an angel. The body of Binks is now trampled by everyone who walks into Heaven.

```
[PLANETJACKPOT_7@iMac-G3 - % cd EXT_DRIVE
[PLANETJACKPOT_7@iMac-G3 - EXT_DRIVE % ls
                    STORIA              STORIB              STORIC
                    STORID              STORIE              STORIF
                    STORIG              STORIH              STORII
                    STORIJ              STORIK              STORIL
                    STORIM              STORIN              STORIO
                    STORIP              STORIR              STORIS
                    STORIT              STORIU              STORIV
                    STORIW              STORIX              STORIY
                                                            STORIZ
[PLANETJACKPOT_7@iMac-G3 EXT_DRIVE % cd STORII
[PLANETJACKPOT_7@iMac-G3 - STORII % ls
                    FATIMA_1            FATIMA_2            MIRACLE_1
                    MIRACLE_2           RAQUEL_1            RAQUEL_2
                    UMA_1               UMA_2               V_1 V_2
[PLANETJACKPOT_7@iMac-G3 STORII % cd MIRACLE_1
[PLANETJACKPOT_7@iMac-G3 - MIRACLE_1 % ls
                    B                   COHEN               KURT SM
[PLANETJACKPOT_7@iMac-G3 MIRACLE_1 % cd COHEN
[PLANETJACKPOT_7@iMac-G3 - COHEN % ls
              GROCERIES             HOLIDAYS                TIMESHARES
[PLANETJACKPOT_7@iMac-G3 COHEN % cd TIMESHARES
[PLANETJACKPOT_7@iMac-G3 - TIMESHARES % ls
                    1_HARD_WAY          1_WOLF_OVAL         3_ROACH_ALY
                    5_CANOE_AVE         6_PROMETHEUS_RD     13_ORIPHUS_CIR
                    33_DEAKIN_RD        77_BRAVOS_SQ        127_ZAPATA_BLVD
                    392_OMEGA_BLVD      1388_OHM_RD         266_171ST_ST
                    US_901_MILE_MARKER_0                    THE_ANNEX
[PLANETJACKPOT_7@iMac-G3 TIMESHARES % cd . . .
[PLANETJACKPOT_7@iMac-G3 COHEN % cd HOLIDAYS
[PLANETJACKPOT_7@iMac-G3 - HOLIDAYS % ls
                    01-JAN-17-2001      02-FEB-02-2001      03-MAR-01-2001
                    04-MAR-02-2001      05-MAR-03-2001      06-MAR-04-2001
                    07-DEC-31-2001      08-DEC-31-2003      09-JAN-07-2004
                    10-JAN-07-2004      11-JAN-14-2004      12-JAN-21-2004
                    13-JAN-28-2004      14-FEB-04-2004      15-FEB-11-2004
                    16-FEB-18-2004      17-FEB-25-2004      18-MAR-03-2004
       19-MAR-10-2004     20-MAR-17-2004    21-MAR-24-2004  22-MAR-31-
                                      2004  23-APR-7-2004   24-APR-14-2004
                    25-APR-21-2004      26-APR-28-2004      27-MAY-05-2004
                    28-MAY-12-2004      29-MAY-19-2004      30-MAY-26-2004
                    31-JUN-03-2004      32-JUN-21-2004      33-JUN-22-2004
                    34-AUG-15-2004      35-SEP-13-2004      37-OCT-01-2004
                    38-OCT-15-2004      39-OCT-21-2004      40-OCT-24-2004
                    41-DEC-31-2004      42-AUG-20-2005      43-SEP-25-2005
[PLANETJACKPOT_7@iMac-G3 HOLIDAYS % cd 43-SEP-25-2005
[PLANETJACKPOT_7@iMac-G3 - 43-SEP-25-2005 % ls
127_ZAPATA_BLVD.raw
[PLANETJACKPOT_7@iMac-G3 43-SEP-25-2005 % cd 127_ZAPATA_BLVD.raw
    Inside the hole of the impaled. A gummy ring around the impaler.
```

She, the impaler. Blood emerging in a self-generating regurgitation, from within and beneath, the ocean's tide, accumulating and being set free to drain and soak. The stiletto black, eternally. Comfortably on the even ground. Tension and torque left behind.

The blood camouflaged with its flesh, at the nascent of its congealment process. The mouth cannot be seen. The smile is hidden behind intention. Pain is intercepted and absorbed. The stiletto through the hole. The hole through the tongue. The tongue prostrate in submission. The tongue harnessing the pain into prostration. Screaming became stillness. The toes covered by black. The stiletto refusing to be bloodied. Some day, a soon hour, faded red footprints in a marble hallway.

```
[PLANETJACKPOT_7@iMac-G3 43-SEP-25-2005 % kill cd 127_ZAPATA_BLVD.raw
[PLANETJACKPOT_7@iMac-G3 43-SEP-25-2005 % cd . .
[PLANETJACKPOT_7@iMac-G3 HOLIDAYS % cd . . .
[PLANETJACKPOT_7@iMac-G3 COHEN % cd GROCERIES
[PLANETJACKPOT_7@iMac-G3 - GROCERIES % ls
           BACLOFEN.txt       CLOBETASOL.txt        DRAMAMINE.txt
           FETZIMA.txt        HYDROCHLORIDE.txt     IBUPROFEN.txt
           JOLLYPOP.txt       KERYDIN.txt           MECLIZINE.txt
           NEURONTIN.txt      ORABASE.txt           PROMETHAGEN.txt
           SPORANOX.txt       TADALAFIL.txt         U-CORT.txt
           THIZZ.txt          VARDENAFIL.txt        WARFRARIN.txt
           YERVOY.txt         ZULRESSO.txt          ZZYVOS.txt
[PLANETJACKPOT_7@iMac-G3 GROCERIES % cd SPORANOX.txt
admnstrd: 01.07.2004/02.04.2004/03.03.2004/04.07.2004/05.05.2004/06.03.2004/10.24.2004
```

prps: dul use / fx vary; c blw

rprt_1: initl use fr fngl nfctn / nddl toe / lft ft

dsg_1: 200ml pr pll / 1pll 2 tms pr day / 12 dys on; 5 dys off / oral; rctl / tkn w/ no sprvsn

fx: mnml aftr 4 mnths / rngng in ers / frqnt urntn / no dsr 2 cntinu

rprt_2: Sbsqnt dsr 2 attmpt agn / intrst in hllcngnc co-fx xplnd upn initl cnfrnc

dsg_2: 200 ml pr pll / 10 plls 1 tm pr dsrtn / dsslv in lqd / tkn undr sprvsn of MIRACLE / nte: crnt stf incldd no ngtve ftrs othr thn typcl dprssn nd usge occrd w/in THE ANNEX.

fx: T+0:15 initl itchng acrs bdy / T+0:27 slw mvmnt nd cgntn / T+0:33 usr dscrbd lss of sptl recgntn w/ rmvl frm prsnt tme nd apprnc of bckwrd mvmt wthn mmry / T+1:01 vrtgo / T+1:08 vmtng / T+1:21 frst hllcntn - "strngld w/ blt" / T+1:39 vmtng / T+1:58 dp slp w/ usr dscrbng 0 drms / T+3:16 vmtng / T+3:18 scnd hllcntn - "suckd n2 cmptr "/ T+3:35 fll bdy crmps / T+3:47 "etrnl blss" w/ coaglnt rltns

rprt_3: usr rqstd 2 pr w/ DRAMAMINE nd NEURONTIN / fx unkwn / exprmntn agrmnt sgnd

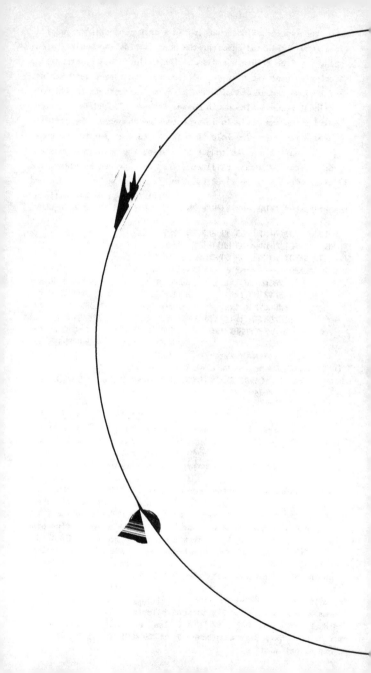

dsg 2: 200 ml pr pll / 8 plls 1 tm pr dscrtn / dsslv in lqd / tkn undr sprvsn of MIRACLE / prd w/ 1800mg NEURONTIN (600mg pr pll / 3 plls / see altrnt rprt 4 prvs use) nd 600 mg DRAMAMINE (100mg pr pll / 6 plls / see altrnt rprt 4 prvs use) / nte 1: pr usr dscrtn, 600 mg SPORANOX addd w/ 600mg NEURONTIN addd "2 nhnc fx n2 altrnt rlm" / nte 2: usr crnt stt incldd mnr indgstn nd ftgue nd use occrd w/in hme rsdnce-13 ORIPHUS CIRCLE

fx: T+0:04 nasea / T+0:11 vrtgo / T+0:14 usr syncpe, MIRACLE plcs bdy flt / T+0:35 usr rspnds 2 stmli / T+0:51 hllcntn 1 - "lrg msss of bnnies" / T+0:56 fll bdy crmps / T+0:59 mnml ablty 2 use xtrm- ties / T+1:09 enggd w/ coaglnt rltns lstng apprx 4.5 hrs / T+6:43 hllcntn 2: "vbrtng mgntc fld of impldng wht dwrf outsde rim of irn plnt" / T+7:43 mvmnt rttrns, accmpnd by apptte / T+10:17 hllcntn 3: "vbrtng urn" - shrt span nd pssbly unrltd 2 usge

ntes: usr xprnce imprvd upn sbsqnt dsge / futr cnsdrtns - mrge dsg w/ 13 drps Vtmn A n ordr 2 cntract dhdrtn nd pssble mcs mmbrn dcayl thrgh hllcngne crse w/ frthr addtn of 400mg - 600mg of CE- LECOXIB n rdr 2 offst dysnrrhea / synthsz via cmpnd srvcs rcmndd 4 ftre use 2 dstll fx nd achv fnl utpia / whle cthrss mght b achvble

I WOULD LIKE TO BE SWIMMING inside this cement bulwark. The ability of inexactness and sedimentality to make perfect is astonishing. And the cheers go again. He's burning worms left and right. I swear, he's going to go to Luton Town or Churbley City. Europe takes the best of us and spits us out. He'll come back miserable and then be even more miserable. I need sauerkraut for my stomach. I can subsist on shredded vinegarized cabbage. "Shut up, Roque." The menu stares back at me. And now her, how has she ended up behind me? I wanted it to happen this way. If push came to shove, I'd do it. I want to get close enough to give myself the choice. I like to feel the temptation and pretend I'm scared of it. I'm the royal clown. "He's scored again," I say to myself and her and whoever else is listening to me whisper. "He scored again," she says. "How do you think he did it this time?" . . . "Hmm, what about a Rabona? He's a Rabonarista." She flips her hair back. She says "Jenny, remember?" and doesn't say anything else about Son of Boris. Jenny isn't important, her name isn't important, not to say names aren't important—because they are, in fact, there's nothing else more important— but it's only important and vital to note that she did it, she said her name's Jenny to me, because what's most important, in this infinitesimal moment, is what else she says, what she says after she claims herself, the fact of her saying it when she did making it the most important, what else she tenderly says with a hint of fear and excitement and panache. Mr. Ricky's boyfriend is huffing spray paint out of a plastic bag under the stands. We're all standing under a daymoon. Roque parked in front of a church and somehow it became a house. Those kinds of circumstances. She says she met De Sade's great-great-grandson and he refused to acknowledge his lineage. I tell her being a De Sade doesn't make one sadistic. Being a text doesn't make one textual. And vice versa, being metropolitan doesn't make one a metropolis. So on, so forth, etcetera. She asks me to show her my hands. I apologize for the blisters. "Some kind of zen lesions," she says. "I must not let it destroy me," I respond. Mr. Ricky's boyfriend breathes heavily inside and out, collapsing his accordion ribs. Jenny brushes my palm and says, "What we try to keep hidden is the most important thing about us." Therein lies the superstructure. I turn my palm clockwise and rotate it back and forth upon the vertical plane. The creases form a monument to future civilization. The pointed tip of ascension and the skinny shaft of connection between our rubble and the wars of the heavens. Roque wants to see and I say no. My wrinkles will become divine. So she tells me. The halftime buzzer sounds. We walk to another food stand to buy tacos. Jenny and Roque converse in pseudonyms. Mr. Ricky's boyfriend crawls down the steps backwards on all fours to find Mr. Ricky. Son of Boris would be checking his shin-guards right now and making sure the money hadn't gone anywhere. I sit down on a metal bench and watch the birds. The images of birds with their heads engorged by plastic rings. I'm imagining the fetish inside a bird's brain. I'm watching Roque talk. He's the funniest person who ever lived but I've never heard him say anything funny. It takes amazing human restraint. I'm poking around my insides on the bench. Coffee will counteract the bacteria. I'm the plastic-eating fungi. Finally, they have discovered me. I'm the ten thousandth planet from the sun. I'm overdosed on Vitamin D. The bird poop etched into the concourse in perfect geometric circles. Spherical hegemony. That's what football is. What is the world telling us about itself and to do about itself and in itself and about us within it? I love you, it says, at first. Wittengensteinen says it, so he says. I hear the whistle piercing the veil. Poor Son of Boris. No, no. No. Poor fans of Son of Boris. *Son-of-Boris, clap-clap-clapclapclap. Son-of-Boris, clap-clap-clapclapclap.* Can he hit a post squarely in its ass, just once? Jenny next to me and Roque next to me and the birds all around us eating fries and hemophytes. Let's go to dinner and have a restaurant. Let's pretend to be still. Let's be mothers. Let's become sick together. Let's go look for the end. Let's stay awake for days. Let's die and leave a scholarship in our name. Let's go back to school and drop out and go back. Let's color our hair different colors. Let's scream very loudly until our heads feel painful. I want to verse out. I want to verse out so far away. "Let's go run amok," I say. "Get in the car and drive to a crater or desert or some geographical semi-deformity." ... "We don't have a car." ... "The world is passing us by." ... "Because of computers." ... "We have tents." ... "Anything is a tent." Jenny laughs. "I will be settled down with another woman when I'm 41," she says. "We'll live in a poolhouse in Mallorca, under the patronage of a cinephile who thinks I look like Lucille Ball and we'll swim in the sun. Our house will have rounded clay roof tiles and the outside will be made of stucco. None of this post-modern bullshit in sight. The small differences make it breathable. We'll still watch football but we'll be very far away from the games, watching on our battery-operated antenna TV, and we'll try to find replays of Maradona because Napoli will be our Mallorca after we've made it to Mallorca, after we've lived inside of it for a while. I like the idea of small triangular flags filling the air. The pool deck will be bright white and will bake us well. I will have lots of money by the time I'm 41, but I won't need it, and that's the best thing you can ask for when it comes to money. I won't drink at all. Hydration is very important." Roque nods. "I'll never step foot on a plane or in a car ever again. 41 is the new 35 is the new 16. Modern science made it so and the cutting edge of it all is in a pool-house in Mallorca with my partner and our dying patron and under the chlorinated water that keeps us clean." ... "You'll miss the weather." ... "The changing of the seasons? Oh sure, of course, I'll miss everything. Even the things you hate you end up missing, because your body needs the matching opposite emotion to make pleasure feel pleasurable. I'll be 40 and found in a ditch and then I'll be 41 in Mallorca and we'll chase the daylight and work to try and forget things we remember and remember things we forget so we can live the life we want to." Roque passes gas and I laugh. There are no clouds in the sky and I decide it's not blue. God is dormant in the expanse. We should go back and collect our line drawings. I think it's time. Mr. Ricky and his boyfriend gallop towards us. The baby has finally learned to walk. The truth aligns, he's a coward. All of Mr. Ricky's shitty blockbusters failed because he made them cast his dumb boyfriend as an alien. My alien is full of heretics, not Mr. Ricky's boyfriend. Roque is lighting a fire. If this was Europe, if we were back in Belgrade, I'd have a smoke bomb. Mr. Ricky looks like he probably owns several guns. He migrated here, eventually, as it happened. Jenny smiles. She's thinking about Spain and the endless future.

"Someone make big big mistake."

"..."

"Big big mistake."

"..."

"..."

"You're lucky. Much richer men than me would pay to defile you."

"Ha."

"That's funny. You're right. That's funny. See my hands coiled into balls? These things can really mess you up if they're used slowly. Tenderly."

"..."

"So you're back, then."

"..."

"Do you feel cold?"

"..."

"I don't think so."

"Carlos."

"Would you like to be eaten?"

"..."

"..."

"..."

"Would you like to live on through me?

"..."

"Would you like to accompany me to the den? Would you like to meet the people I spend time around? Would you like to see the melting faces laughing with me? Would you like to see a priest and a butcher and a doctor and a Marxist and a diplomat and a banker and a junkie and a comic strip artist and a ship captain and a botanist? Would you like to play chess with them? Would you like them to threaten you, each in their own special way? Would that feel good to you? Would you like them to stick a cross in your ass, a dollar bill, a stethoscope, a cell phone, a meat cleaver, a handful of hair, a syringe, a vial of ink, a plank of wood, a cactus? Would it make sense to you if I told you they like the world to be wet? Would you like to settle like spoiled milk? Would you taste good, I wonder? Would you volunteer yourself? Is that what you've already done? Would you like to die by poetry? Would you remember any of this if you died again? Would you like to pretend to feel warmth? Would you like to stagger upon my smoke? Would you like to meet the real me, the me I have concealed from myself? Would you like to introduce us? Would you be able to give me an inkling of what comes ahead? Would you like to receive veneers? Would you prefer to shit out your intestines? Would you like to be cut and wait for the blood to never come? Would you please reveal the Lord? Would you please reveal my Lord? Would you sit upon my leather as I feed on you? Would you give up your favorite food to become a God? Would you give up your favorite food to try at love again? Would you like to go by Roach? Would you like to go by Boron? Would you like to go by Nuno or Brian or Abdul? Would you like to go by Carlos? Would you like to go by Carlos? Would you like for that to be something that you could do?"

"..."

"..."

"Big big mistake. Carlos. Big big mistake."

"Would you like to be dipped into the house wine and cured and be made brethren of the Almighty?"

"..."

"Would you like me to tell you how lucky you are, you lucky little shit? And so the atoning hands of God have become your tongue and upon it He preaches to sip delicately for now there is more than one way to enter and He hath made it so."

"Ah."

"Now you see. Now you see, don't you?"

"..."

"..."

"Carlos."

"..."

"Carlos make big big mistake."

"..."

"Big big mistake."

"..."

"..."

"..."

"Carlos. Where I go?"

"Mmm. Would you like to see the rooms behind the room?"

"..."

"Would you like to see the portal of a thousand fetuses stranded in the mucus of time?"

"..."

"..."

"Body hurt."

"I believe your formaldehyde-dipped-body would contribute to my high."

"..."

"But would you believe me if I told you there was no such thing as a body?"

"..."

"..."

"..."

"Would you like me to tell you more about the pervert?"

"..."

"Are you at home in the pervert?"

"..."

"In the pervert we are home."

"..."

"The pervert hides in the open because he can. The pervert has realized the world does not deny him. The pervert wishes the world would deny him. The pervert slams the buttons on the machines, but his fingers are soft. The pervert is no longer aroused by the bells and whistles and flashing lights. The pervert no longer hears the whacking of the solid carbon steel. The pervert has been playing pinball for over forty years, and when one does a thing for a span of decades, he becomes comfortable and the thing he loves becomes not the thing he is doing but the thing behind the thing he is doing . . . "

```
[PLANETJACKPOT_7@iMac-G3 - % cd EXT_DRIVE
[PLANETJACKPOT_7@iMac-G3 - EXT_DRIVE % ls
                STORIA          STORIB          STORIC
                STORID          STORIE          STORIF
                STORIG          STORIH          STORII
                STORIJ          STORIK          STORIL
                STORIM          STORIN          STORIO
                STORIP          STORIR          STORIS
                STORIT          STORIU          STORIV
                STORIW          STORIX          STORIY
                                                STORIZ
[PLANETJACKPOT_7@iMac-G3 EXT_DRIVE % cd STORIN
[PLANETJACKPOT_7@iMac-G3 - STORIN % ls
                IVEY_1          IVEY_2          JENNY_1
                JENNY_2         SUKI_1          SUKI_2
                        VICTORIA_1      VICTORIA_2
[PLANETJACKPOT_7@iMac-G3 STORIN % cd JENNY_1
[PLANETJACKPOT_7@iMac-G3 - JENNY_1 % ls
                        COHEN           KOSMOS          MISTER
                        NIJS            UDO             VICIOUS
                                                        WADE
[PLANETJACKPOT_7@iMac-G3 JENNY_1 % cd UDO
[PLANETJACKPOT_7@iMac-G3 - UDO % ls
        GROCERIES               HOLIDAYS                TIMESHARES
[PLANETJACKPOT_7@iMac-G3 JENNY_1 % cd HOLIDAYS
[PLANETJACKPOT_7@iMac-G3 - HOLIDAYS % ls
01-SEP-28-2001
[PLANETJACKPOT_7@iMac-G3 HOLIDAYS % cd 01-SEP-28-2005
[PLANETJACKPOT_7@iMac-G3 - 01-SEP-28-2005 % ls
66_GATES_JUNCTION.raw
[PLANETJACKPOT_7@iMac-G3 09-28-2005 % cd 66_GATES_JUNCTION.raw
```

A flexed calf muscle hanging in the air. The connected foot ejected
   out of the frame. The rim of a white, sleeveless undergarment
   hugging a shape of flesh. There are no hands. A sawed-off bed-post
    in the hazy background. A metallic cellular phone plugged into
    the wall, dangling by a cord. Everything is suspended. Light from
    mid-day sun or midnight streetlamp extending through the window.
    All parts illuminated without intention. The long night of the
   Northern Hemisphere or an eternal day of Heaven. A stack of Gideon
   Bibles. Impenetrable curtains set in layers. A blank alarm clock.
    The single leg weaved into the shadows. The calf muscle tessel-
   lated. Something on the wall. A bug on the ceiling or a hiccup in
    the capture mechanism. A stain on the wall. A ripple in the green
    wallpaper. A reflection projected from the outside world. A smile
   in the vapor. An impossibly visible emptiness. A number written on
   the wall. A letter written on the wall. An intentional fingerprint.
                            A mite of dust on the screen.

```
[PLANETJACKPOT_7@iMac-G3 01-SEP-28-2005 % kill
cd 66_GATES_JUNCTION.raw
```

MAYBE SHE WOKE UP, maybe she spent some time in the bathroom looking at herself in the mirror, maybe she didn't feel like eating breakfast but knew she should and ate a sleeve of Saltines, maybe she read a newspaper she found lying on the table and purposely didn't look at the date so she could feign ignorance, maybe she drank a glass of cranberry juice, maybe she went back into the bathroom and ate a handful of technicolor antacids, maybe she looked at the clock and put on a black bikini and walked to a coffee shop and ordered a black coffee and filled it with cookies n' cream creamer and sipped it while she waited for the old man with dark voids in his eyes to come talk to her in a soft voice, talk to her about the way the world worked, maybe she flirted with the barista before she left, maybe she stopped at Peg's or Dad's on the way home and bought a bag of cheese curls, maybe she saw a woman with long black hair loving her from afar, maybe she thought about how she would like to finish the filmography of Nicolas Roeg, maybe she waited at the bus stop and said damnit when she realized she forgot her headphones, maybe she wanted to run to the library and steal a book of poetry, maybe she never read poetry before, maybe she got on the bus and heard the voice of the intercom talk about cities that never sleep and how every day could be your last and maybe she wondered out loud how those could be true, maybe she got off the bus at the lake, maybe she sat in the vertex of a dune and ate her cheese curls and dropped one and covered it with sand so that no one would ingest her mistake, maybe she waded into the water and perched on a rock and pretended to be a sea lion, maybe she walked to the concession stand and tapped on the window even though the sign said it was closed, maybe she waited around for a while on a swing, maybe she got into a nice car, maybe that car drove the long way back to the city, maybe the car dropped her off at a library but maybe she didn't want to go in, maybe she wanted to watch the filmography of Éric Rohmer, maybe she talked to a man sitting on a bench in front of a fountain in the library's courtyard and she held his hand, maybe they joked about how he bit his nails down to the cuticle, maybe they walked up the fire escape and maybe they laid together on her couch, maybe she woke up again, maybe she went to the bathroom, maybe she looked in her fridge and closed the door and then opened it again, maybe she walked to the small home office of a doctor and asked him what this and that meant, maybe she thought about watching the filmography of Pedro Almodóvar, maybe the wood-paneled furniture and fuchsia carpet triggered a memory of a photo of her aunt and uncle's living room in New York City, maybe she wanted to fall asleep to a good film, maybe she walked by a sandwich shop and stared at the menu and maybe she almost ordered a turkey club sandwich before leaving, maybe she placed a call on her cellphone and talked for a couple blocks, maybe she placed another call and left a message after the automated voice, maybe she sat on the marble steps of a bank and smoked two cigarettes, maybe she thought about the long-haired woman from the corner store and how the long-haired woman goes home at night and watches shows on BBC with her friends and drinks hard liquor and loves her cat named Chumdog and reads books about nature on her Kindle and sleeps in a large t-shirt and does not sleep very well and wishes she could find a pillow to make her neck not feel so sore and eats oatmeal with berries in the morning and drives to work on time and takes smoke breaks every three hours and hates working in front of screens and eats fast-food for lunch and texts her mother only once a day out of duty and wishes she could do something other than what she is doing in that exact moment and remembers she would feel the same way if she was doing something else and eats a ginger chew and looks at the clock and tries to avoid her co-workers and eats another ginger chew and clocks out a minute early and drives to the YMCA and plays racquetball well and sits in a wood sauna for twenty minutes and talks to an acquaintance about a natural disaster in Bolivia and changes back into her work clothes and pets her cat back at home and watches *Jaws* by herself and feels a spiritual connection to Quint and wonders how long after the events of the film would Quint have killed himself if he hadn't been eaten by a shark and thinks about what she would look like with glasses and throws away her birth control and dissolves a sweet white pill on her tongue and eats potato mash and drinks a ginger ale and pours a can of Chumdog's wet food onto the floor and lays down in bed with her feet hanging off the side and stares at the twenty-seven glow-in-the-dark plastic stars on her ceiling and wishes she had bought a set of planets too and makes herself yawn to try and trick her body into being tired and gets up to turn the TV back on in the living room and leaves it on a low hum and gets back in bed and thinks about how her neck will feel in the morning and wonders how much a specialized bed would cost and if a warmer climate would help and maybe an Epsom salt bath if she had a bathtub and she closes her eyes and opens her eyes and closes her eyes and crosses her arms and thinks about the girl with the red hair.

THE CAR IS OUTSIDE AGAIN. The Chrome Falconer. Wi-Fi network: OnceBeloved. The clock is broken again and still. Roque continues. "We should take down these mirrors." Many streets converge here. For lunch I ate candy-coated droplets and vegetable soup and coffee. I was in Paris just hours ago. All of the streets and roads converge here. My friend Roque peels back the tapestry curtain, brittle like parchment paper. Chrome hurts me. I was just in Paris yesterday. If I was in Paris, I wonder what it would've been like. Paris changed around me to fit me. The Eiffel Tower is not so tall. It's diminutive. "Roque!" He likes to listen to 100.0 FM – The Sphinx. That's what we call it. Wi-Fi network: Raoul's iPhone (3). "I'm not a drug addict. Don't joke about that." ... "They're in fashion." ... "They're unprotected." ... "We're unprotected." ... "It's 11:11. Make a wish." ... "Okay. I will." ... " ... " ... "I swear I'm going to." ... "Okay." ... "Okay." ... " ... " ... "Here we go." ... "And then, the wish." ... "Okay. I will. Believe me, I will. I'm thinking. I've actually thought about it but I'm re-thinking. No, double-checking." ... "Here we go." ... "Okay." My mouth is dry and the car is still outside. Inside, in between the two front seats, there are two beings, oddly shapeless and discordant. And roadkill on the driveway. The bright wave breathes. The silhouette of a single beer bottle slants into unknown circuitry. Roque is eating a bowl of cereal and trying to find the local news on the TV. He has always been friends with the one newscaster and he hates the weatherman. Everyone hates the weatherman. Personally and professionally. I miss Paris. The radio there is beautiful because I can't understand anything so it all takes the shape of music, even the channels where they talk and talk and talk about grapes or explosions or whatever it is the French deem important enough to throw out into the universe. "Roque!" We both love static, it's not just him. Every horror movie begins and ends with static. I'm going to stare at the car until it leaves our house. I'm going to read a book a book about syntax. There are stories everywhere if you pretend everything is a story. "Turn the radio up, Roque." The static on the radio mixes nicely with the static on the TV. Two different kinds of shifting and crinkling. The softness of sand and the harshness of a vacuum. They offset one another. Roque and I like to bring people over when the static is playing, just to watch their eyes. Another thing we like: the static in a set of eyes. The man walked from a couple blocks away, I don't know how many and I couldn't say where he started from, maybe he came from the place itself, but I know he didn't drive, how do I know it, well I know it, I feel it, I don't think he would drive to meet the driver, him, the formless shape inside the other shape, and I don't know why they would meet here, except for the fact that all of the avenues converge here. The city is a traffic circle and there's only one exit. I was in Paris tomorrow. I don't mind being watched. I cannot mind being watched because I'm watching, and I don't do things I wouldn't want to be done to myself. The Golden Rule they taught us in school and said to never forget and said was the most important lesson, more important than anything else we would learn in any class. In the cafetorium, they said it. The cafegymtorium. The same place we watched a magician, a man of the incongruent arts. The newscaster speaks in King James' English. Hilarious death and all its accoutrements. The visage of kabuki-men. And whatnot. Reckoning yips. The hymn she's singing belongs to no god. A long passage, this is what TV has become. I'm obsessed with word counts. Find the formula, different than a code, misshapen compared to a rhythm, the same vein as a pattern, uninterpretable and foundational since we were all one atom. "Roque, turn the TV down and the static up." They would like to hear this. All three men are shaped now and looking out the car window towards me. I don't think they're talking. I hope they aren't talking. Roque and I aren't talking, so it wouldn't be fair. She left me the tone. I practice saying "she left me the tone." We're staring at the eight-foot-tall porcelain sasquatch behind our TV. Roque says cancer is a black bike in the middle of the night. Either cancer is the black bike or cancer is on a black bike. But it's definitely in the middle of the night. Why do things smell like shit and what is the smell of shit? They never leave the car and go into the house, but I know they're here because of the house.

Everything converges here and is squeezed into this place. Okay, the man is walking away. He's wearing a hat and I've never seen him in a hat and hoodie and jeans and I'll always be able to recognize him even though he's dressed like everyone else. Listens to an old cassette tape while walking. Listens to anxiety, not the sounds of anxiety or a song of anxiety or words of anxiety, he listens to anxiety. Step off my lawn, sir. No, property belongs to everyone, something something something land is universal. The car is leaving. How can a book written in the past about our present become our future? "Roque, turn up the TV. We must hear the news. We must be informed citizens." Wifi network: None Found.

I

("I'm thinking about the inevitability" ... "the evolution, elimination" ... "of the language of the mind, my engrained prose" ... "the obliteration and silence" ... "until we are reduced to a single word" ... "suffocated" ... "or nothing at all" ...)

```
[PLANETJACKPOT_7@iMac-G3 01-SEP-28-2005 % cd   . . .
[PLANETJACKPOT_7@iMac-G3 HOLIDAYS % cd   . . .
[PLANETJACKPOT_7@iMac-G3 UDO% cd   . . .
[PLANETJACKPOT_7@iMac-G3 JENNY_1 % cd   . . .
[PLANETJACKPOT_7@iMac-G3 STORIN % cd JENNY_2
[PLANETJACKPOT_7@iMac-G3 - JENNY_2 % ls
                                                                    DOOR_1
[PLANETJACKPOT_7@iMac-G3 JENNY_2 % cd DOOR_1
[PLANETJACKPOT_7@iMac-G3 - DOOR_1 % ls
                                                                    DOOR_5
[PLANETJACKPOT_7@iMac-G3 DOOR_1 % cd DOOR_5
[PLANETJACKPOT_7@iMac-G3 - DOOR_5 % ls
                                                                    DOORWAY_1
[PLANETJACKPOT_7@iMac-G3 DOOR_5 % cd DOORWAY_1
[PLANETJACKPOT_7@iMac-G3 - DOORWAY_1 % ls
                  DOOR_15              DOOR_16              DOOR_17
[PLANETJACKPOT_7@iMac-G3 DOORWAY_1 % cd DOOR_15
[PLANETJACKPOT_7@iMac-G3 - DOOR_15 % ls
                                                                    DOORWAY_2
[PLANETJACKPOT_7@iMac-G3 DOOR_15 % cd DOORWAY_2
[PLANETJACKPOT_7@iMac-G3 - DOORWAY_2 % ls
                                          DOOR_33              DOOR_34
[PLANETJACKPOT_7@iMac-G3 DOORWAY_2 % cd DOOR_34
[PLANETJACKPOT_7@iMac-G3 - DOOR_34 % ls
                  DOOR_63              DOOR_64              DOOR_65
[PLANETJACKPOT_7@iMac-G3 DOOR_34 % cd DOOR_65
[PLANETJACKPOT_7@iMac-G3 - DOOR_65 % ls
            DOOR_111             DOOR_112             DOOR_113
                                                      DOOR_114
[PLANETJACKPOT_7@iMac-G3 DOOR_65 % cd DOOR_111
[PLANETJACKPOT_7@iMac-G3 - DOOR_111 % ls
                                      DOORWAY_4            DOORWAY_5
[PLANETJACKPOT_7@iMac-G3 DOOR_111 % cd DOORWAY_4
[PLANETJACKPOT_7@iMac-G3 - DOORWAY_4 % ls
                                      DOORWAY_8            DOORWAY_9
[PLANETJACKPOT_7@iMac-G3 DOORWAY_4 % cd DOORWAY_9
[PLANETJACKPOT_7@iMac-G3 - DOORWAY_9 % ls
                                      DOOR_175             DOOR_176
[PLANETJACKPOT_7@iMac-G3 DOORWAY_9 % cd DOOR_175
[PLANETJACKPOT_7@iMac-G3 - DOOR_175 % ls
            DOORWAY_19           DOORWAY_20           DOORWAY_21
                                                      DOORWAY_22
[PLANETJACKPOT_7@iMac-G3 DOOR_175 % cd DOORWAY_21
[PLANETJACKPOT_7@iMac-G3 - DOORWAY_21 % ls
                                      DOOR_260             DOOR_261
[PLANETJACKPOT_7@iMac-G3 DOORWAY_21 % cd DOOR_260
[PLANETJACKPOT_7@iMac-G3 - DOOR_260 % ls
                                      DOOR_368             DOOR_369
[PLANETJACKPOT_7@iMac-G3 DOOR_260 % cd DOOR_369
[PLANETJACKPOT_7@iMac-G3 - DOOR_369 % ls
DOOR_504         DOOR_505
[PLANETJACKPOT_7@iMac-G3 DOOR_369 % cd DOOR_505
```

```
[PLANETJACKPOT_7@iMac-G3 - DOOR_505 % ls
               DOOR_665          DOOR_666                     DOOR_667
     DOOR_668          DOOR_669               DOOR_670 DOOR_671
[PLANETJACKPOT_7@iMac-G3 DOOR_505 % cd DOOR_671
[PLANETJACKPOT_7@iMac-G3 - DOOR_671 % ls
                                       DOOR_869              DOOR_870
[PLANETJACKPOT_7@iMac-G3 DOOR_671 % cd DOOR_870
[PLANETJACKPOT_7@iMac-G3 - DOOR_870 % ls
                                                        DOORWAY_51
[PLANETJACKPOT_7@iMac-G3 DOOR_870 % cd DOORWAY_51
[PLANETJACKPOT_7@iMac-G3 - DOORWAY_51 % ls
                                                        DOOR_1105
[PLANETJACKPOT_7@iMac-G3 DOORWAY_51 % cd DOOR_1105
[PLANETJACKPOT_7@iMac-G3 - DOOR_1105 % ls
                                                        DOOR_1379
[PLANETJACKPOT_7@iMac-G3 DOOR_1105 % cd DOOR_1379
[PLANETJACKPOT_7@iMac-G3 - DOOR_1379 % ls
                          DOORWAY_127           DOORWAY_128
[PLANETJACKPOT_7@iMac-G3 DOOR_1379 % cd DOORWAY_127
[PLANETJACKPOT_7@iMac-G3 - DOORWAY_127 % ls
                          DOORWAY_322           DOORWAY_323
[PLANETJACKPOT_7@iMac-G3 DOORWAY_127 % cd DOORWAY_323
[PLANETJACKPOT_7@iMac-G3 - DOORWAY_323 % ls
                                                        DOOR_1695
[PLANETJACKPOT_7@iMac-G3 DOORWAY_323 % cd DOOR_1695
[PLANETJACKPOT_7@iMac-G3 - DOOR_1695 % ls
             DOORWAY_833          DOORWAY_834           DOORWAY_835
[PLANETJACKPOT_7@iMac-G3 DOOR_1695 % cd DOORWAY_835
[PLANETJACKPOT_7@iMac-G3 - DOORWAY_835 % ls
                                                        DOORWAY_2188
[PLANETJACKPOT_7@iMac-G3 DOORWAY_835 % cd DOORWAY_2188
[PLANETJACKPOT_7@iMac-G3 - DOORWAY_2188 % ls
               DOOR_2055            DOOR_2056                DOOR_2057
[PLANETJACKPOT_7@iMac-G3 DOORWAY_2188 % cd DOOR_2056
[PLANETJACKPOT_7@iMac-G3 - DOOR_2056 % ls
           DOORWAY_5788         DOORWAY_5789           DOORWAY_5790
    DOORWAY_5791      DOORWAY_5792       DOORWAY_5793 DOOR-
WAY_5794       DOORWAY_5795          DOORWAY_5796         DOORWAY_5797
                    DOORWAY_5798        DOORWAY_5799 DOORWAY_6000
[PLANETJACKPOT_7@iMac-G3 DOOR_2056 % cd DOORWAY_5798
[PLANETJACKPOT_7@iMac-G3 - DOORWAY_5798 % ls
                    DOOR_2463         DOOR_2464            DOOR_2465
[PLANETJACKPOT_7@iMac-G3 DOORWAY_5798 % cd DOOR_2465
[PLANETJACKPOT_7@iMac-G3 - DOOR_2465 % ls
                                                        DOOR_2925
[PLANETJACKPOT_7@iMac-G3 DOOR_2465 % cd DOOR_2925
[PLANETJACKPOT_7@iMac-G3 - DOOR_2925 % ls
                    DOOR_3436            DOOR_3437            DOOR_3438
                    DOOR_3439            DOOR_3440            DOOR_3441
[PLANETJACKPOT_7@iMac-G3 DOOR_2925 % cd DOOR_3439
[PLANETJACKPOT_7@iMac-G3 - DOOR_3439 % ls
                                                    DOORWAY_15511
```

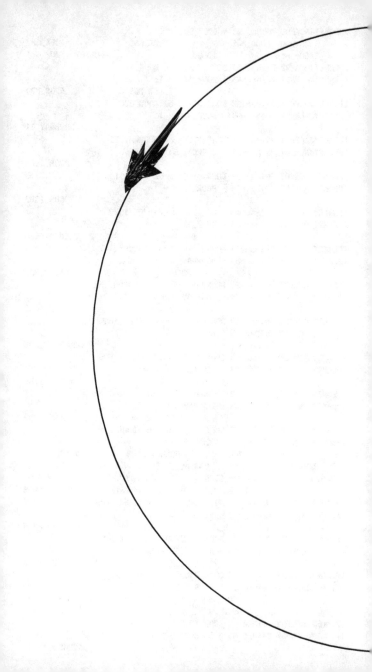

```
[PLANETJACKPOT_7@iMac-G3 DOOR_3439 % cd DOORWAY_15511
[PLANETJACKPOT_7@iMac-G3 - DOORWAY_15511 % ls
                            DOORWAY_41834       DOORWAY_41835
[PLANETJACKPOT_7@iMac-G3 DOORWAY_15511 % cd DOORWAY_41835
[PLANETJACKPOT_7@iMac-G3 - DOORWAY_41835 % ls
                            DOOR_4009           DOOR_4010
[PLANETJACKPOT_7@iMac-G3 DOORWAY_41835 % cd DOOR_4010
[PLANETJACKPOT_7@iMac-G3 - DOOR_4010 % ls
                                                PUTRIFICATION
[PLANETJACKPOT_7@iMac-G3 DOOR_4010 % cd PUTRIFICATION
[PLANETJACKPOT_7@iMac-G3 - PUTRIFICATION % ls
                                                DOOR_4641
[PLANETJACKPOT_7@iMac-G3 PUTRIFICATION % cd DOOR_4641
[PLANETJACKPOT_7@iMac-G3 - DOOR_4641 % ls
            DOORWAY_113632   DOORWAY_113633    DOORWAY_113634
[PLANETJACKPOT_7@iMac-G3 DOOR_4641 % cd DOORWAY_113634
[PLANETJACKPOT_7@iMac-G3 - DOORWAY_113634 % ls
                                    DOOR_5335           DOOR_5336
[PLANETJACKPOT_7@iMac-G3 DOORWAY_113634 % cd DOOR_5335
[PLANETJACKPOT_7@iMac-G3 - DOOR_5335 % ls
                                                DOORWAY_310572
[PLANETJACKPOT_7@iMac-G3 DOOR_5335 % cd DOORWAY_310572
[PLANETJACKPOT_7@iMac-G3 - DOORWAY_310572 % ls
                    DOOR_6095       DOOR_6096           DOOR_6097
[PLANETJACKPOT_7@iMac-G3 DOORWAY_310572 % cd DOOR_6095
[PLANETJACKPOT_7@iMac-G3 - DOOR_6095 % ls
                    DOOR_6924       DOOR_6925           DOOR_6926
[PLANETJACKPOT_7@iMac-G3 DOOR_6095 % cd DOOR_6924
[PLANETJACKPOT_7@iMac-G3 - DOOR_6924 % ls
                                DOORWAY_853466      DOORWAY_853467
[PLANETJACKPOT_7@iMac-G3 DOOR_6924 % cd DOORWAY_853467
[PLANETJACKPOT_7@iMac-G3 - DOORWAY_853467 % ls
DOOR_7825
[PLANETJACKPOT_7@iMac-G3 DOORWAY_853467 % cd DOOR_7825
[PLANETJACKPOT_7@iMac-G3 - DOOR_7825 % ls
                                                BASEMENTS
[PLANETJACKPOT_7@iMac-G3 DOOR_7825 % cd BASEMENTS
[PLANETJACKPOT_7@iMac-G3 - BASEMENTS % ls
MOTHER.txt
[PLANETJACKPOT_7@iMac-G3 BASEMENTS % cd MOTHER.txt
```

> Thirty-five children later
> She doesn't exist
> This is the year
> 2066

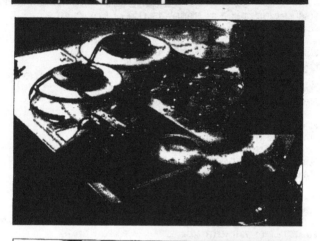
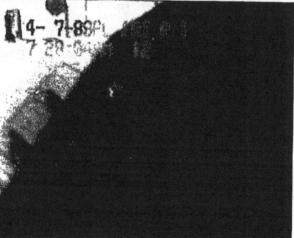